Still the One

an Oyster Bay novel

Olivia Miles

~ Rosewood Press ~

ISBN 978-0-9995284-6-4

STILL THE ONE

First Edition: February 2019

Still the One

an Oyster Bay novel

Chapter One

Melanie Dillon was having a "day." She had them several times a week lately, now that wedding season was approaching. Things would start off fine enough. Coffee. A shower. Sometimes just a dry shampoo. Another coffee. She'd take a brisk walk to her shop, where she was usually the first to arrive, something she preferred as she settled into her routine: fluffing tulle veils and dress skirts, straightening jewelry displays, looking over the appointment book, and checking order status sheets. Soon Chloe, her business partner and cousin, would arrive. Then Sarah, their newest hire. And then…the brides.

It was the brides who were the problem. (Well, when it wasn't their mothers, sisters, future mothers- or sisters-in-law, or friends.) She knew she could never admit it. Not to Chloe, whose entire life was Bayside Brides, and not to Sarah, who just loved all things weddings, and not to her brother, who was getting married in two weeks and whose fiancée was a client of the shop, of course. She couldn't even tell her own mother, who was already worried enough about her "attitude" of late. Not anyone. The brides were the clients. The brides kept the lights on, the doors open, and their reputation in Oyster Bay and the surrounding towns positive.

But Melanie was having a day.

She realized with a start that it was only eleven, meaning really, the day had only just started, but given the hysterical crying coming from the dressing room, you would have thought today's client was planning a funeral instead of a wedding. Melanie and Sarah locked eyes across the room and, deciding that her assistant had it covered, Melanie slipped away. The storage room was cool and dark and she closed the door behind her, relishing the solitude as she pulled a melting square of milk chocolate from her blazer pocket. She unwrapped it quickly and slipped it into her mouth, closing her eyes until it had completely dissolved on her tongue.

There. Three soothing breaths and she was ready to face Mindy Henderson again, whose attempt at going on a new fad diet hadn't yielded the results she'd hoped for.

"There's still time," she heard Sarah say softly as she walked into the storefront, but all Sarah received in response was a loud snort followed by a fresh bout of tears.

Melanie felt her blood pressure rise and she grabbed her handbag from behind the appointment desk before she said something she would come to regret, like how really, Mindy was still quite thin, and having a dress taken out rather than taken in was unconventional, yes, but given the state of the world, was it really such a crisis? After all, Mindy was getting married. She had met someone who loved her. Who wanted to spend his entire life with her.

It was more than she could say for any of the employees of the store.

Well, damn. Her heart went all heavy again and the pity weighed down her steps as she motioned to the door. "I'll grab us lunch while I'm out. Abby Harper's dress is due to arrive today and I want to swing by the post office to make sure I have it before her appointment this afternoon."

Sarah looked disappointed but nodded. "I'll have a turkey on wheat. No mayo. And no cheese."

In the three-way antique mirror, the bride glanced over her shoulder and let out a strangled scream when she saw that the buttons could not be fastened all the way up her back.

Sarah's eyes burst open at the sound. "Make that a tomato and brie," she said with a sigh.

Make that two, Melanie thought, as she pushed out the door onto Main Street.

Her first stop was Angie's, Oyster Bay's most popular

café, where she didn't even need to look at the menu to study her options. Leah, the newest hire, set both sandwiches into a paper bag and added a double chocolate fudge cookie on the house.

"You looked like you needed it," she said.

So the day was looking brighter, Melanie thought with a smile that lasted all the way to the post office, where sure enough, Abby's dress was boxed and waiting on a shelf for the afternoon delivery. Scratch that one off her list.

"It won't go out until the four o'clock run," Kitty said, pulling a face.

Melanie tucked the bakery bag into her oversized tote. "That's okay. I'll take it now." She was just as eager to see the dress as she knew Abby would be. With the wedding only two weeks away, they were pushing it close, but of course the dress that Abby liked had to be special ordered, and made, and it had certainly taken her long enough to decide on the style she liked. After she had tried on every dress in the shop. Twice.

Kitty pulled the large box from the shelf and set it on the counter. "Something else arrived for you too." She gave Melanie a strange look. Her eyes roamed up and down her body.

Melanie frowned. "Well, if it's not too big, I can take it now. Otherwise, delivery will be fine."

Kitty patted her white, bordering on blue, tinged hair and pinched her lips. Without a word, she pulled a box out from under the counter and set it on top of the one containing Abby's duchess satin wedding gown, complete with a six-foot train.

Melanie glanced at the return address with passing interest, but her cheeks flooded with heat when she saw the name in bold. She looked up, locking Kitty's knowing eyes, and felt the blood drain out of her face. It wasn't supposed to be like this. She was supposed to place the order, have her items delivered, all within the wonderful autonomy that came with online shopping.

Except that she lived in Oyster Bay. Where everyone knew everyone. And their business too.

"Are congratulations in order?" Kitty asked, her left eye starting to twitch as she continued to stare at Melanie.

"Must be a mistake," Melanie said briskly.

"Oh?" Kitty didn't look convinced. "Well, we can return it to the sender. What was it again?" She pulled her reading glasses from the chain around her neck and peered down at the label. "Everyday Maternity."

Now Melanie was the one with the pinched lips. She darted her eyes around the post office, tittering away her anxiety. "No need to trouble yourself. I'll just…save it as a gift. Or…something."

"Nonsense! Clearly there was a *major* misunderstanding. I'll start the label and take care of everything." Kitty began typing at her computer screen.

Melanie felt her shoulders sag. She'd been looking forward to these new clothes since she'd placed the order last week, in the private solace of her apartment, after her jeans had threatened to cut off the circulation of her midriff. She didn't even know why she'd thought of it. Maternity clothes? When she wasn't even pregnant?

Kitty triumphantly printed the label and pulled the sticky sheet from the back. She hovered with her hands over the box, as if calling Melanie's bluff, waiting to see if Melanie would cave, stop her, admit that she had indeed ordered two pairs of elastic-waist jeans, three forgiving blouses, and elastic-waist dress slacks in three professional shades.

"So…you're sure you won't be needing these?" Kitty asked carefully.

Melanie gathered the wedding dress box from the counter, managing its bulk awkwardly as she headed to the door. "Not unless it's an immaculate conception," she muttered, and the look on Kitty's face made that rather sad revelation almost worth it.

*

Melanie managed to get the box back to the store and through the door, warily glancing around the room for a hint of the tearful bride to be.

"She's gone," Sarah said without needing to be asked.

"Good," Melanie said, dropping the wedding dress box onto the counter. "She's bad for business!"

Sarah just shook her head as she took her sandwich from the open bag Melanie offered. "Is that a cookie in there?" she asked hopefully.

Melanie had been looking quite forward to that cookie,

knowing just how rich and fudgy they were, but seeing as she'd be squeezing into her too-tight jeans this weekend, or admitting defeat and buying a size (or two) up at the store, she happily handed it over to Sarah. Sarah was thin and blonde and yet she also struggled in the romance department. And really, Sarah was the one who actually wanted to get married, whereas Melanie…Melanie didn't know what she wanted anymore.

Peace. Quiet. A killer metabolism. A day without a woman who seemed to have it all complaining about how wrong everything in her life was, leaving Melanie to wonder what that woman would think of her life, if she were to share?

But that would be bad for business. After all, who would want to buy a wedding dress from this sad lot?

They had a strict policy about food and drinks in the storefront, so Sarah took her food to the back room, and Melanie propped open the door to join her. They rarely had drop-ins on weekdays, and their next appointment wasn't for half an hour, and that was Abby, practically family, or soon to be.

"Do you think we'll be at the singles table?" Sarah asked as she took a hearty bite of her sandwich.

Melanie thought of the elastic-waist pants that were now on their way back to the sender, and sighed as she unwrapped her lunch.

She was always at the singles table. When she wasn't at the head table, that was. And considering that she and

Sarah were both bridesmaids in Abby and Zach's ceremony, the odds were a fifty-fifty split. Not all brides did head tables anymore, and Abby was breaking code and holding her wedding at the Oyster Bay Botanic Garden instead of at the Harper House Inn, where both her sisters were married last year. It was a popular wedding destination, and, thanks to Melanie's connections with the facility manager, and more than a bit of rubbing up to Dottie Joyce, head of the Historical Society which oversaw the maintenance of the Garden, she had been able to fit Abby and Zach in last minute.

Honestly, who got engaged on New Year's Eve and then wanted a spring wedding with all the bells and whistles?

But that was just like Abby. She didn't always think things through.

One could only hope she had given some attention to the seating arrangements, for the lonely hearts in town, at least.

From the storefront, the door jangled the wedding bells that hung from the frame by a blue velvet ribbon. The bells had been there since she and Chloe first opened the shop seven years ago, and despite the other changes they had gradually made to the storefront, the bells never changed.

Melanie poked her head through the opening from the storage room and grinned back at Sarah.

"Ask Abby about the table configurations if you want. She just walked in."

"I will if I get a moment. I have to call back Dorothy Whiting, and you know how demanding she can be."

Melanie did. She crammed another bite of her sandwich into her mouth and chewed quickly. The last thing she needed was for Abby to see her eating something from Angie's, even if her rivalry with the place had dissipated now that she had a permanent gig at the inn and was no longer threatened that if she messed up, her sister would replace her delicious breakfasts with pastry options from the café.

Melanie set her sandwich to the side to finish later. She was quite eager for Abby to see the dress, twirl with joy, and finally put an end to the wedding gown saga. With the wedding only two weeks from tomorrow, she hoped to have the dress pinned for any last-minute alterations within the next week. There was always something so satisfying when a bride finally found the one—the one dress that was everything she ever wanted and couldn't exactly describe in words. It was something more subtle, more subconscious. It had to be felt.

"I know I'm early," Abby's eyes were wide as they scanned the room. "I couldn't sleep last night knowing the dress was arriving today. It is…here, right?"

Melanie gave a knowing grin and walked behind the counter to fetch the scissors from the drawer. "I waited for you before I opened it. Ready?"

Abby let out a breath but nodded excitedly. "This is it!"

It. Such a simple word that had come to mean so much in the bridal industry. "It" was right up there with "the one." The man. The dress. The venue. The color scheme.

You knew "it" when you saw it. At least, some women did. Others had to be guided, ad nauseum and ad infinitum, she thought, eyeing her soon to be sister-in-law.

Carefully, she cut through the tape that sealed the box and set the scissors back in the drawer. She'd learned the hard way that you could never be too careful with sharp objects in the storefront, after Madison Kroller's flower girl cut the sash on her wedding dress when everyone was distracted by a heated veil discussion (one layer or two?). Fortunately, Melanie was able to convince Madison that colored sashes were trending, and, after consulting the flowers in her bouquet, she'd whipped up a lovely peach satin sash quicker than Madison's tears could dry.

Still. Better safe than sorry. And the last thing she needed was anything happening to Abby's dress. Not when they'd finally found "the one."

Ever so slowly, she lifted the flaps from the box and pulled back the tissue paper, barely believing what she was seeing. No. No, no, no, no.

"That's not my dress!" Abby's voice was shrill. Then, with a hand to her heart, she gave a grin. "That must be another order. I got scared for a minute there."

Not as scared as Melanie was. Her heart was thudding as she picked up the order form and scanned it. Abby had specifically chosen a crisp white satin and this was an antique ivory. Maybe Chloe had placed a similar order for another bride. Or maybe this was a sample from a designer.

Or maybe that was all just wishful thinking.

"It says right here that it should be made in the white satin." She frowned at Abby, who looked on the verge of tears. "Do you want to try it on anyway? You never know until you see it in the mirror." But she knew that there was no way Abby would like it. Abby wanted white. It was a spring wedding. She'd made all this very clear in her many, many appointments.

"We just got some new arrivals," Melanie suddenly remembered. She forced a smile and hurried to the rack near the jewelry case, fumbling through the hangers until she found the dresses.

Abby shook her head at each one. "I can't believe this," she said, groaning as she dropped onto the blue velvet armchair and sank her head into her hands.

Melanie could believe it, unfortunately. By the wedding day, everything usually righted itself, presenting the perfect picture that each bride longed for, but the journey to that moment was bumpy at best. And it was her job to fix a crisis, like the big one, the one happening right now.

"I'll call the designer," she said, walking back to the counter and picking up the phone. "Maybe they have your dress. They probably just sent the wrong one."

But one look at it told her otherwise. Abby had chosen

to customize the original design by asking for a sweetheart neckline and some extra beading at the waist. "Or they can make it again. I'll ask for a rush order."

Abby stood and came over to the counter, frowning down at the dress that was still in the box. "You know," she said slowly, and Melanie stopped dialing the phone. She stared at Abby, her breath locked in her throat. She knew that tone. That hesitation.

Doubt. Abby was having doubts. And that was never good.

"I'm not so sure this neckline works with the dress after all."

Melanie realized that she was glaring at her friend, who was a client, after all. A difficult one, but all the same, a client. "Why don't you try it on?"

Abby shook her head. "No. Nope, it won't work. The color is all wrong and the neckline." She ran her fingers over the edge of the bodice, where it met the skirt. "I'm not feeling these beads either. I thought they'd be smaller. It all seems a bit heavy for a spring wedding."

Given that Abby didn't "feel" any of the hundred options they carried in the store at any given time, Melanie struggled to hide her frustration. She glanced at the storage room, looking for some back-up, but Sarah's voice could be heard on the phone: "Of course, Mrs. Whiting. But white for a mother of the groom is not as common as you may think."

She turned back to Abby, hoping to reason with her. "If you just try on the new dresses. The ball gown with the crystal covered spaghetti straps is my personal—"

Abby wrinkled her nose. "I'm sorry, Melanie. I like a lot of them. But I like parts of them, not the whole dress. And this neckline." She grimaced as she looked down at the dress in the box. "I don't want a sweetheart neckline after all. Too much...cleavage."

Right. That did it. Clearly there was no point in asking them to send another dress in the correct fabric. Privately, Melanie knew there wouldn't have been time anyway, not with the wedding so soon.

She closed the box and taped it shut. Moving on. Another trip to the post office, she thought, dragging out a sigh.

Abby wandered around the store, sighing and shaking her head. "I just don't think I'd be truly happy with any of these. I mean, they're gorgeous, but they just aren't...me." She stopped suddenly and eyed Melanie from across the room. "Unless..."

Melanie didn't like the sound of this. "Unless?"

Abby was wringing her hands as she approached the counter. "Maybe you could make a custom dress for me?"

A custom dress. Melanie didn't know whether to feel excited or horrified. Her gut instinct crept in and she blurted, "No." She cleared her throat. "I'm sorry, but I don't think there's time and..."

Besides, she hadn't sewn an entire garment in years. Alterations, sure. But a gown was a huge undertaking. And a lot of pressure. And who had the time?

"Please?" Abby was gripping her hands now. "What else am I supposed to do? I know you can sew and I've seen your sketches too."

"When?" Melanie said. No one saw those sketches. She made sure of. She kept them in her nightstand drawer for that exact reason.

And because she didn't want to look at them either. Or think about them.

"The last time I was at your apartment!" Abby smiled. "You told me I could borrow your gold hoop earrings, so I went into your room looking for them."

And she saw the book. Melanie pulled in a sigh. It was a hobby, nothing more. A dream, perhaps. And one that had been shelved many years ago.

"That's a very old sketchbook." She hadn't even looked at it in…Years, she realized with a frown. Once it had been in her bag at all times. She couldn't fill the pages quickly enough.

"I know you could make me the perfect dress," Abby insisted, her eyes full of hope.

Melanie wavered. She looked down at the taped up box, wondering if she even had a choice. And Abby was practically family, and would be soon enough.

"It could be your gift to me," Abby said, biting her lip.

Damn, the girl should have been a lawyer, not a cook at the Harper House Inn, Melanie thought. "I'll think about it."

"Meaning that's a yes." Abby could barely suppress her squeal.

Knowing she was going to regret this, Melanie shook her head. "It means I'll think about it." But with the wedding quickly approaching, she couldn't think about it for long, and Abby knew that just as well as she did.

"I just know you're going to say yes!" Abby ran around the counter to give her a hug, a really, really tight one. "This is going to be the best wedding ever!"

Melanie was happy that Abby's arms were still gripping her neck so she wouldn't see the trepidation in her face.

Best wedding ever? She needed some wood to knock on and quick.

Chapter Two

It had become a tradition since Sarah started working at the shop that on Friday nights, they went out for drinks. It started early into their time together, when it became clear that the single girls had to stick together, because more and more of their friends would claim plans with their husband, fiancé, or boyfriend, or bring them along, and that just changed everything. After all, they couldn't exactly discuss their man troubles, poor eating habits, or thoughts on new hair styles with a guy sitting at the table.

Well, they could if the guy happened to be Jason Sawyer, best friend extraordinaire, who was finally back in town after more than a year. When he'd first moved to Boston, he'd claimed he'd return every weekend. But then life got in the way. Melanie supposed it always did in the end.

"So much for tradition," Sarah said as they stepped through the door of Dunley's.

"Jason's different," Melanie said as she scanned the room. "He's my oldest friend. We can talk about anything with him. Believe me; he's heard it all from me over the years. You're going to love him."

Sarah perked up. "Is he cute?"

Melanie frowned at this. Sarah was always on the prowl, and it wasn't often a new face showed up in Oyster Bay other than a summer tourist, but Jason? That just felt…complicated.

"Jason is married to his work," she said, and that wasn't a lie. When he'd graduated from med school, he'd wasted no time taking an opportunity at a hospital in Boston, his visits becoming less and less frequent, and even their phone calls and video chats becoming shorter. More often than not those chats took place in the break room, and often he was interrupted by someone needing his assistance with a patient. It was admirable work, of course, but selfishly, Melanie had been thrilled when Jason announced he was coming back to fill in for his dad while he recovered from a heart attack.

The room was crowded—there weren't too many hot spots in Oyster Bay, after all, and this gastro pub was topping the list—but she knew he'd beat them here. Jason was always on time, almost annoyingly so, and he prided himself on it. He was reliable. A man of his word.

"What does he look like?" Sarah asked, and something in her tone told Melanie that her motivation stemmed from more than just wanting to help spot him.

"Tall, dark hair, brown eyes, may or may not be wearing a doctor's coat." Although, probably not. He had only just arrived in town today. The clinic in town had been closed all week since Mr. Sawyer's heart attack last Friday. It had been mild, thankfully, but he'd spent the weekend at St. Francis Hospital all the same, Jason monitoring the situation from Boston since he couldn't get away until now.

"A doctor!" Melanie heard Sarah sigh just as she spotted him, there, at the end of the room, studying the menu that was posted on an oversized chalkboard that hung from the far wall.

No white coat. Just a blue linen shirt rolled up at the sleeves instead. And just like that, all the stress from the day, all the stress from many days, actually, just rolled away and all seemed right with the world again. Jason was back.

"Jason!" She couldn't be sure he heard her across the crowded room, but of course Jason never failed.

He looked over at her, his face breaking out into a huge grin that made her heart feel like it could burst right then and there, and she hurried across the room to him, where he pulled her into a bear hug. His chest was as familiar as his scent and she hadn't even realized how much she'd missed it until now.

"Don't stay away so long next time," she said, pulling back to let Sarah step forward.

Jason gave a boyish grin. "I just need a reason to stay."

"Last I checked your dad just had heart attack. Isn't that reason enough?"

"It was mild. He's recovering." Jason shrugged, but Melanie knew him well enough to see the worry in his eyes. He looked tired. And he hadn't shaved in a couple days. It was a look that suited him, she thought.

Not that she'd be feeding that ego anytime soon. Working in a trauma center had gotten to his head quite enough in recent years, from what she'd noted. Not that she could blame him. He'd gone out and done what he'd always dreamed of, exceeded it really, far beyond the confines of this small hometown. She couldn't exactly say the same, could she?

"Well, I'll give you a reason to stay," she said, and she saw Sarah's eyes pop with interest. Melanie frowned again. No, not that! "I happen to have had the absolute worst year of my life, and if you were here it would have been, well, not so bad."

"Not so bad." He laughed. "That the best you can do?"

"Well, I did get dumped last Valentine's Day, as you know. I'm not a total robot. I do have feelings."

"Are you commenting on my bedside manner again?" He gave her an appraising look, but she saw his mouth twitch.

"I didn't say a word," she said, struggling not to roll her eyes. She saw how he was on their video chats, speaking of his patients in perfunctory and overly scientific terms. She could only hope he hadn't done the same when his father was in the hospital last week. But then, Dr. Sawyer had a few decades more of experience under his belt and probably wouldn't tolerate that kind of talk.

"Hey," he said, laughing again. "You said I would have made the last year all better if I'd stayed."

She hadn't said *all* better, but actually, the truth was that it would have been all better if he'd been here. Everything always was. "We both know that when it comes to practicing medicine, you are a walking textbook. I still don't understand how you can be one person in real life and another in your professional life."

"Says the woman who drinks wine out of a box yet encourages her clients to drop two grand on a dress they will only wear once?"

"Good point!" Sarah joined in, laughing now.

"I'm sorry. I've lost my manners." Melanie shook her head. She was getting carried away. It tended to be this way when she and Jason were together. Time passed and it was as if the world around them stopped. Or didn't matter. Or both. But tonight was Friday night, girls' night, and she stood by her girlfriends. It was a promise she'd made to herself once the others starting drifting off, one by one. Men came and went, but the women in her life, they were golden. "This is Sarah Preston. She moved to town while you were off saving lives in Boston and now she works for Bayside Brides."

"A pleasure," Jason said, shaking her hand.

Melanie watched the exchange with mild amusement. Sarah was pretty, with blonde hair and big blue eyes, but she was also eager, and it tended to scare men off. Jason, however, seemed painfully oblivious. It was probably why he hadn't had a girlfriend in, well, never, unless you counted the sporadic dates or casual flings as girlfriends, and she knew he didn't.

"Should we get a table or brave the bar?" Jason looked from Sarah to Melanie, happy to let them have their way.

It was standing room only and Melanie wrinkled her nose as she searched for three possible stools. It looked like a couple was just standing to leave (Amanda Quinn was still dating Joe?) and Melanie went to claim the spot when she saw *him*. There, next to Amanda, or at least the place where Amanda had been sitting, was Doug McKinney. Her Doug. The Doug who had dumped her on Valentine's Day last year.

"What's wrong?" Jason asked, perhaps sensing that she had lost the ability to speak or move and that she wasn't even sure she was breathing. Doug didn't come here. He never came here. She made sure of it. It was the one place she could feel comfortable showing up to on a Friday night, not having to worry about sliding back into the land of the dead and depressed, where she'd lived for months after the breakup.

"What is he doing here?" she heard Sarah hiss.

"He?" Jason turned and looked. "Oh. Doug."

"Shh!" Melanie felt her whole body go stiff. The last thing she needed was for Doug to think that she still cared. Because she didn't. Of course she didn't. But damn it, she did. Why else would she feel like she was about to break out in a sweat and she couldn't even remember where the exit was or how to run to it?

"Someone should tell him to leave," Sarah said. "This is our bar."

"It's a free country," Melanie said sadly. Usually Doug went to The Lantern, at least that's what her friend Evie had told her—she'd spotted him a few times when she was helping her dad run the bar. But now it seemed he was mixing things up.

"We'll go," Jason said.

"Go where?" Sarah pointed out, and it was true. There were only a few bars in town and all would be packed at this hour, worse once summer came. As part of the Main Street renovation, they were expanding the street for commercial zoning, and there was talk of a few new restaurants and shops opening, but that didn't exactly solve tonight's problem.

And it was supposed to be such a great night.

"Let's go anywhere. Anywhere but here," Melanie pleaded. She wasn't prepared for this. She wasn't looking her best. Sure, she had seen Doug. It had been over a year and Oyster Bay was tiny. There was no avoiding him, but Lord had she tried. Usually she was able to dodge him, see him coming and dart the other direction. Find out he was attending an event and skip it. But mostly she stuck to her routine, and he stuck to his, and that worked. Until tonight.

"It's been a long time," Sarah surprised her by saying. "And I think he saw you. If you run out of here now, he'll know you still care."

It was a good point. Still, she wanted to do just what Sarah was telling her not to do.

"Do you still care?" Jason asked, looking at her with a strange expression.

She glanced back in Doug's direction. He was with Matt Gordon, an old buddy. Not a girl. She had heard rumors he was seen with Jessica Paulson lately, but here it was, Friday, and he was alone.

And she liked that. And she shouldn't. Because she cared. And she shouldn't.

Damn it.

"Come on," Jason said. "A table just opened up, and I have a feeling that you could use a drink."

Make that two, she thought as she followed her friends to the back of the room. But still, just having Jason at her side, she felt better.

*

They managed to get a table at the back of the room, and Melanie took a chair that allowed her to sit with her back to the bar. Jason ordered a round and eyed Doug over her shoulder, gritting his teeth with disgust. If he could, he'd march over there and take a swing at the guy, or at the very least, exchange a few choice words. But what was done was done, and it had been over for quite some time.

Melanie, however, did not appear to be over it at all.

"Doug McKinney was always a jerk. I can't believe you ever even went out with that guy."

Who could forget the time he'd toilet papered the principal's house, just for a few good laughs? Sure, he'd been a punk teenager back then, but he'd been a punk as a kid too. Judging from Melanie's story, he hadn't shown any signs of change.

"He was fun," Melanie said lamely.

"And cute," Sarah offered, with a shrug. But she winced a little, and Jason gave her a little smile across the table. Yeah, she got it. Doug was a jerk. He hoped she'd stressed that to Melanie, too, although judging by the tension that remained on Melanie's face, Sarah hadn't fared any better than he had.

The drinks came up quickly, and Jason took a long sip of his beer, grateful that the clinic was closed for the weekend and he wouldn't have to step in to his father's role until Monday. That was one perk to being back in town—no overnights, no weekends, no twenty-four-hour shifts. He'd spent the afternoon at his childhood home, cramming his clothes into his childhood drawers, trying to squash the guilt he felt at his mother's overt joy to have him back.

It was only temporary, but she didn't seem to believe that. He'd felt guilty about coming out tonight, but after a few hours with his parents, he needed the escape. His father was recovering well, and in no time he should be able to get back to work. His boss had given him a two-week leave, and only because he had accumulated so many unpaid vacation days.

"Enough about me. How's your dad? Your mom must be a wreck!" Melanie shook her head as she reached for her wine glass.

Jason took a long pull on his beer. His mother was a wreck. Of course she was. She'd aged ten years in a week and he could tell she hadn't been sleeping much, either. No amount of reassurance would put her mind at ease. But having Jason back, she'd said, was just the cure they both needed.

He closed his eyes briefly. He was so much more comfortable discussing other people's problems than thinking about his own.

"Nice try, but I'm not finished discussing your love life."

"Or lack thereof," Melanie said with a heavy sigh.

Jason leaned into his elbows on the table. This close to Melanie, he could see the light dusting of freckles on her nose. She hated those as a kid. Tried to scrub them off. Even asked his dad once if there was a cure. He'd liked those freckles, told her so, made her smile, and she'd never complained about them again. He still liked them.

Liked what they reminded him of. Liked what they made him feel.

"So what did you see in Doug other than that he was fun and reasonably attractive? You know that isn't exactly a stellar descriptive for a long-term match."

Melanie rolled her eyes. "I enjoyed my time with him."

"Until he broke your heart. On Valentine's Day." He shook his head, finding it hard to believe that even Doug could be that big of an ass. He vaguely remembered the details of his calls with Melanie around that time. He had one of the interns nagging him about some test results in the background. "He really did it on the day?"

Sarah nodded solemnly, her eyes round. "On the day."

"I thought we were going to dinner. He said he'd come by around seven. I bought a new dress and some jewelry from the shop and everything. But he showed up in jeans and a hoodie."

"A hoodie!" Sarah wrinkled her nose. "You never told me that part before."

"Too ashamed," Melanie said, shaking her head sadly. "He didn't even have a single flower or a box of chocolates. And there were no reservations."

"So you stood there all dressed up…" Sarah looked horrified.

"And he told me that he just didn't feel like we had enough of a connection to move forward. Then he left. I heard he was at The Lantern that night, drinking beer, laughing with some of the guys…"

Jason stared at Melanie, who let out a long sigh. Right. Enough of the self-pity. She may have gotten away with it for the past year, but she was right about one thing, and it wasn't ever accepting a date with Doug. If he had been here, the last year would have been different, and she sure as hell wouldn't be sitting here on a Friday night, more than a year after a breakup, hiding from a guy who never deserved her in the first place.

"Level with me here. Did you ever really think that Doug was the guy you were going to marry?" He raised a finger when she went to open her mouth. "Ah. No. And don't you even try to tell me that you're not looking for husband material here. It's me, Mel. I know you want to settle down. There's nothing wrong with that."

She pursed her lips. "Says the guy who has never dated a girl for more than a month,"

"Hey, I'm being fair here. I'm not going to lead a girl on. I've been sleeping at the hospital five out of seven nights for the last two years." He set his beer down. "Seriously, though, you want to get married. So why do you keep going out with guys who don't?"

"I don't know!" Melanie said, tossing up her hands. She turned to Sarah who seemed equally baffled.

"Don't look at me," she said, taking a sip of her wine. "I'm just as hopeless as you are."

"Seriously, though," Jason said, facing the women. "You are both attractive, easygoing, intelligent women."

Sarah blushed, and Melanie frowned at her. "And far too susceptible to the slightest bit of flattery," she said.

She and Jason shared a smile. They got each other like that. "If you're looking for a guy that's going to stick around, who wants to settle down, not just have a little fun, then maybe should be looking for someone a little less…smooth."

He'd sat back and watched Melanie fall for it year after year, guy after guy. There was Josh back in ninth grade, then Keith in tenth. And who could forget the guy after college? It was the same story every time. The same type of guy, just a different name.

"Smooth?" Melanie cocked an eyebrow.

"Face it, Mel," he said with a smile. "You like the bad guys."

"I do not!" Melanie scoffed. "I just…Oh, whatever."

Jason leaned back in his seat, argument won, but somehow the victory wasn't felt.

"Changing topics, I had some interesting news today," Melanie said, after their second round of drinks was delivered to the table.

"Really?" Sarah perked up and leaned into the table. "What kind of news?"

Jason was also eager, and anxious, because too many times he'd seen Melanie's plans end in disappointment. He saw it coming, sometimes from the onset, and sometimes gradually, and happy as he was to be there for her when things came crashing down, he'd much rather see her happy.

"Abby asked me to make her wedding dress."

"What about the dress you picked up today? The custom order?" Sarah shook her head. "I knew I should have come out and said hello. I got busy with phone calls in the back room and I was so fed up by the time I got off the phone with Dorothy Whiting that I was afraid I would spoil the happy moment if I showed my face. She is still insisting on wearing white to her son's wedding! Claims it is *off* white. Wants me to place the order!"

"Well, it was far from a happy moment," Melanie said. "The dress came in ivory instead of white, but even if the fabric had been correct, I don't think it would have lived up to Abby's expectations. She doesn't like the bodice, or the beadwork. I have to say that I agree with her. It was never the right choice."

"It's amazing how tough she's been to please," Sarah remarked. "She's usually so easygoing."

Melanie shook her head. "She's always been indecisive. And picking out a wedding dress can turn even the most confident buyer into a doubtful mess."

Usually Jason's mind tended to drift when Melanie got to talking about weddings and dresses, but this was different. This was an opportunity, and one that Melanie should seize. "I'm glad the dress didn't work out. You should be making dresses, Mel, not just selling them."

Melanie seemed to waver. "I'm not sure how Chloe will feel about that. She's always been so reluctant to expand the scope of our services. She'd rather stick to the system that works."

"She'll be back on Monday," Sarah said. "You can mention it in the team meeting. And I agree with Jason. It's the perfect chance to grow the business."

"And it's the perfect excuse to get to doing what you love," he said.

"Doing what I love," Melanie marveled aloud. "It's been a long time. It's easier to get swept up with everyday responsibilities."

"Now you sound like Chloe," Sarah warned. "She loves the safe path. Anything that's a sure thing and doesn't lead to any disappointment."

"I *have* been pushing to expand the business," Melanie said, sipping her drink.

"Besides, you don't want to let Abby down," Jason pointed out.

"True," Melanie said, slowly. "She's a friend, not just a client. And she'll be family soon. She said it's the only gift she wants from me."

Sarah's expression turned dreamy. "Don't you just love the idea of a homemade wedding gown in the family? Something that gets passed down through the generations? Something that has a story behind it?"

Jason looked at these two women, wondering if they were for real. Sarah was clearly the perfect addition to the shop, and she'd succeeded in telling Melanie just what she wanted to hear, too.

"Okay. I'll do it." Melanie's eyes popped to underscore her panic, but her smile was straight from the heart.

"See? Everything's looking up," Jason said, giving Melanie a grin.

She met him halfway, uncertainty still in her eyes. "Maybe."

"Positive thinking, Mel!" He told all his patients this; sometimes, when things were bad, it was all he could tell them, all that was within their power, when they were feeling so hopeless and scared. Sometimes it worked. Sometimes nothing worked.

"Yes!" she said. "Yes, everything is looking up! This year will be different."

"I'll toast to that," Jason said.

"Me too!" Sarah said, holding up her glass.

"This time next year, things will be better," Melanie said. They clinked glasses and all took a hearty sip.

Jason had a shifty feeling in his stomach he couldn't quite pinpoint, and he'd been having it all day. Something told him that this year would be different than the last. But he just wasn't so sure that it would be better.

Chapter Three

Weekends were something Melanie had come to dread in the last year. When she wasn't working, they were either filled with social events where she showed up alone, her single status glaring each time as each person in her life paired off, or they were spent in her favorite armchair, in sweats, remote in one hand, bowl of chips in the other, her mind wandering to all the things she wanted to be doing instead.

Either way you looked at it, no good was found. This weekend, however, Melanie started her morning with a list. A short list. A pathetically short list really. Her "this year will be different" list. It included all the things she really wanted. Top of the list? No more pity party weekends. Second on the list: expanding Bayside Brides. Third on the list (and here she hesitated) was finding "the one."

So far she had kept to her list. She'd spent all of Saturday working at the shop, tending to brides (some nervous, some demanding) and reviewing the catalogues for the fall's lines. To her, each dress was prettier than the next, and even though she didn't have to worry about plans for her own wedding, she supposed that was a good thing, because she probably wouldn't be able to ever nail down a date. A spring wedding seemed even more beautiful than a Christmas wedding sometimes. And then a fall wedding seemed more beautiful than a summer wedding.

But Abby's wedding was a spring wedding. And Abby needed something light and simple and unique to her style. Melanie had stayed up until midnight with her sketchbook, and she was excited and nervous to show Abby some of her ideas. She still hadn't committed, not officially, but she had a feeling that if she and Abby could agree to a design, she'd have no excuse to refuse.

And deep down, she wasn't so sure she wanted to. Now that she had dusted off her sketchbook, she remembered how much she had loved it. How each blank page was just waiting to be filled with a new idea.

She sipped her coffee. It was her third cup, thanks to the lack of sleep. She'd decided to cut sugar from her diet, starting today, because she could make no argument for pushing that off until tomorrow, even to herself. The coffee was bitter, but not terrible. And it was a reminder that change was needed. But would it happen? She'd wanted to expand the business for years, but Chloe was more anxious and conservative. And without her partner's support, she was stuck in a holding zone.

But even though her cousin Chloe was still fighting her initiative on the business, somehow expanding the store's services felt more doable than finding a guy who was sweet, funny, cute, smart, and committed.

She knew Jason was right: Doug was a jerk. He'd dumped her on Valentine's Day! And the only time he'd reached out again was to take back some movies he'd left at her apartment. The nerve! And it had been more than a year. She should be over it by now. Instead, she was ten pounds heavier, maybe closer to fifteen, and she hadn't even gone on a date since her last one with Doug. It wasn't even a great date. They'd gone for pizza and he'd had one too many beers and spent the whole night watching the game on the television screen, no interest in conversation. She should have known then that something was wrong. Instead she'd assumed they'd just gotten comfortable with each other.

On Valentine's Day this year, she and Sarah had gone to a fondue restaurant three towns over, in Shelter Port, thinking that it might be a way to get out, meet a few new guys, fresh faces and all that. But they hadn't stopped to think that single men didn't go to a fondue bar on Valentine's Day. Instead, they'd been surrounded by couples, happy couples, and the waitress had assumed that they were one too, something that managed to pull their frowns into smiles, and despite their disappointment, they had laughed the entire way home.

She laughed now, as she stuffed her sketchbook into her tote and checked her watch. The shop didn't open until ten on weekends, but she liked to arrive early and review her appointments for the day. She also wanted to check on the fabric they had in stock, usually reserved for small orders for sashes or swatches. She planned to take a few samples with her when she met Abby at the flower shop after work. As bridesmaids, she and Sarah had offered to help finalize her centerpieces—something that Posy, the shop owner, was thrilled about, given Abby's indecisiveness. She knew Sarah saw it as a golden opportunity to drop hints about the seating arrangements, too.

The weather was warming up, and Melanie slipped into ballet flats and grabbed a cardigan, just in case they stopped at Jojo's afterward for a glass of wine and managed to snag an outdoor table. Wedding season was upon them, although of late every season felt like wedding season. Still, Oyster Bay was especially popular in the summer, when tourists flocked from Boston, New York, and as far away as Philly, for a weekend getaway. Rates at the Oyster Bay Hotel skyrocketed, and the spillover meant the Harper House Inn was filled up, too, another reason that Abby had decided to hold her nuptials at the Botanic Garden. She was a good sister that way. Thoughtful.

And soon she would be Melanie's family. All the more reason to be sure the dress was all that Abby wanted and more. Today, with any luck, she'd firm up the design. Tomorrow she would order the fabric, rush delivery, and the pattern could be made while she waited for it to arrive. It didn't allow much room for error, but the dresses that she had sketched were simple, modern, and suitable to Abby's personality. She wanted something light and airy, sweet and traditional, but not overly embellished. Melanie could do it. She wanted to do it.

She hurried down Main Street, key in hand, when she spotted Jason coming out of Angie's. He spotted her and waved, and the smile on his face made her heart speed up. She'd meant what she'd said the other night. The last year would have been better with Jason in town. Even though he'd been gone for years, Oyster Bay still felt lonely without him and she'd never gotten used to his absence. He'd been a constant fixture in her life growing up, as close to her as Chloe or Zach. He was more than a friend. He was family. She hated the thought of him leaving again in only two weeks. His visits were too short and far too infrequent.

"Hey." He greeted her with surprise in his voice, which was sort of funny, considering you couldn't walk down Main Street without bumping into at least ten people you knew well and the rest that you were at least acquainted with.

Or wanted to avoid. There were several of those actually, not just Doug. Dottie Joyce, town gossip, Bev

Wright, ever eager to set up her son Tim with anyone who was willing to have him, poor thing, and of course, now there was Kitty. Who thought she was pregnant.

Melanie sighed at the thought of those maternity pants… But nope, none of that. Those pants would have been a crutch. And what she needed was a fix! Leave it to Jason to swoop back into town and inspire her.

"What has you up and about so early on the weekend?" she asked.

"You do know that I usually work seven days a week," he reminded her.

"Yes, but now you're in Oyster Bay, not Boston, and the clinic is closed on weekends. Unless you plan on adding extra hours?" The people would be thrilled. Just this winter when Emma slipped on the skating pond and twisted her ankle, Bridget Harper had to drive her all the way to St. Francis to have it looked at because she didn't want to interrupt Dr. Sawyer on his day off. Abby was left to cover the Sunday brunch crowd without any assistance, and she was still worried about that ever happening again, especially as the inn continued to remain full weekend after weekend.

Jason shook her head. "I'm just here temporarily. I'm not here to make any big changes."

"Except for the changes we talked about making," she pointed out. She grinned with the progress she had already made. "Though come to speak of it, you didn't exactly voice what your plans were."

"Well, if you must know," he said, lowering his voice, "I'm waiting to hear if I received a permanent position at the hospital once my residency is up."

She blinked, trying to process what he was saying. He'd gone to med school in Boston and done his internship and residency there, too. She'd assumed it was all part of his studies, held out hope that when all that training was over that he'd be back.

"You mean you want to stay in Boston…indefinitely?"

"I'm a good fit there. I like to think that I can make a difference." His jaw set as he looked down Main Street. "It's been a while since I've been back. Not much has changed though."

"A year ago Christmas to be exact."

He looked at her sharply. "I was on call this past Christmas. And Thanksgiving"

She knew. His parents knew too. She suppressed a sigh of disappointment. "Well, you're right. Nothing has changed around here." Except all her friends and family who were suddenly getting married. Good for business. Bad for morale. And Jason, he hadn't changed at all. Back in school he was always top of the class, and in all the honors classes. He'd finished college in three years instead of four thanks to all his AP credits, and gone straight to med school, as expected, even landed a one-year fellowship at Harvard. Ever since he was a kid he'd talked about being a doctor. Melanie had naively assumed he meant following in his father's footsteps. But then he got the internship in Boston and then, well.

"Oyster Bay is still the same. A few new shops. The same annual events. But the Main Street renovation is still in planning."

"Renovation?" Jason asked.

Melanie hitched her tote higher onto her shoulder. Her sketchbook made it heavier than usual. "They plan to add more benches, expand some sidewalks for more outdoor dining options when tourist season hits, that sort of thing. Some new business too." All good ideas, unless you were to ask Chloe. She'd been fretting about how it would impact Bayside Brides ever since the plans were announced, fearing the construction would deter traffic or that new shops could garner their business. Melanie had pointed out that if their business was affected, then all shops in town would be affected, and that more businesses on the street meant more people would be out shopping, and more people might come into the store, but try telling Chloe that.

Melanie sighed. Chloe had always been this way, ever since they were kids. She was only a year older, but her maturity always seemed to exceed that age gap. When they were younger, Melanie's mother had explained it was because Chloe had to grow up too quickly. Her father was always losing his job, her mother, who was Melanie's mother's sister, had to sometimes take on two jobs as a result. Chloe lacked security, and somehow, she still did.

"I have time to sit if you want to grab a coffee," Jason said, motioning to a bench under a maple tree.

"I can't," Melanie said, her shoulders slumping. "I have to go into work. Chloe's out of town and if today is as crazy as yesterday, I'm in for a long day." The only saving grace was that the shop closed at four on Sundays. She was eager to meet up with Abby and see what she thought of the sketches.

"Dinner this week then?" he asked. "You free tomorrow night?"

She was free every night these days, but even if she wasn't, she would make herself free for Jason.

She only wished lately that she was as much a priority to him as he was to her. But then, she supposed she wasn't the one saving lives, was she?

*

By four thirty, Sarah was trying hard not to lose her patience. Abby had already decided on the flowers two months ago, along with the bridesmaid dress colors. She wanted the entire mood to be simple and elegant, light and happy. The bridesmaids would be wearing pale pink. Emma, the flower girl, would wear white with a pink sash. The groomsmen would wear navy. The flowers would be white roses.

Except now Abby was having a change of heart. "Maybe I should go with something more colorful. A mix of pinks."

Across the room, Sarah saw the flower shop owner look up in alarm.

"You do know this is a first-world problem," Sarah

said. She was off the clock. They were on friend time. Technically, she could say these things without getting in trouble with her bosses. Melanie was a friend, but Chloe…Chloe was a little scary. She could still remember the look in Chloe's eyes the first time Sarah had offered to let a bride try on a pair of shoes without offering up some footies first. Or the time that a flower girl had come into the shop sipping on a juice box. There was a firm no food or drinks policy in the storefront, after all.

"I know," Abby said. "And I never thought I'd be like this. I mean, Bridget…" She rolled her eyes. "You know how particular she can be. And she didn't sweat a thing at her wedding. Same with Margo, but she is more laidback. And she's an interior designer. This stuff comes naturally to her."

"It was the second wedding for both of them," Sarah pointed out. In fairness, she could understand why Abby was being so picky about things. If she ever got married (scratch that negative mentality: *when* she got married) she knew it would be next to impossible to rule out the hundreds of beautiful dresses and commit to just one, to forgo all the beautiful flower arrangements she saw in this shop for just one color scheme or concept. As it was, every time a particularly pretty gown came through Bayside Brides, she snapped a photo of it with her phone, wanting to remember it in case her day suddenly arrived, except now she had at least a hundred photos saved in her device, taking up valuable memory space to boot, and if she were asked to choose just one, right now, well, she probably wouldn't be able to do it.

Still. Abby had committed to an entire concept. And wavering now would only lead to endless regret. She'd seen that already in the short time she'd been at Bayside Brides. The brides who wavered were the ones who were never satisfied and who were always regretting their choices.

"Well, I intend for this to be my first and only wedding. I just want to get it right."

Sarah slipped her a smile. "I understand. So you're thinking of mixing in some color then?"

Abby wandered through the tables of the shop, her eyes darting. "Now I'm thinking of mixing in some daisies. Maybe some lilies…Or…"

No. Just no. Sarah knew what was going to follow that pause.

"Or maybe I should have a colored bouquet and the bridesmaids can carry white."

Sarah glanced desperately to the door. Melanie had been held up with a last-minute fitting, a walk-in fifteen minutes before closing who decided to try on twelve dresses. Twelve!

Even with the delay, she'd expected Melanie to be here by now. And she needed back-up. She needed Melanie's expertise. Melanie had been talking brides off the brink of hysteria for years now with her calm demeanor and tried and true experience, however vicarious. Melanie knew how to get through to them.

Even ones as difficult as Abby, Sarah thought, sliding her eyes back to her friend.

"While we're talking about flowers and centerpieces, are there any single guys you could sit me next to?" She studied an arrangement of daffodils, hoping to keep the eagerness out of her tone.

"Like who?" Abby pointed out. "Tim?" She laughed, but Sarah didn't. After all, Beverly Wright had stopped her at the grocery store twice this winter, asking her about her plans for Valentine's Day. With the Harper and Donovan girls matched up, she was moving on to setting up her son with the remaining single girls in town, and while there were still several of them, Sarah seemed to be the one she currently had her sights on.

The door to the shop jingled and Sarah felt her shoulder sink in relief when she saw Melanie come through the door, her brown hair bobbing at her shoulders, her blue eyes alert and eager. She seemed to pick up on the mood immediately because her eyes flicked to each woman and then to Posy, the shop owner, her smile slipping. "Everything settled?"

Posy's eyes widened a fraction as she set down the stems she was shucking of their leaves. "Almost."

Melanie's lips thinned, and Sarah had to bite back a smile. She supposed there were worse things in this world than having the pleasure of working with your friends every day, even if some of them were driving you nuts.

"We were just talking about the guest list." She looked

at Abby, her exasperation building. "Are you really inviting Tim to your wedding?"

"No," Abby said. She glanced at Melanie. "But do I even need seating arrangements?"

"Yes!" said all three women in the shop simultaneously. It was bad enough that Abby was forgoing the traditional wedding rehearsal the day before the wedding, claiming that she felt a run through would detract from the excitement of the actual event, and pointing out that they had all had enough practice walking down an aisle lately anyway. Sarah also knew that Melanie's mother had lost three nights of sleep over this, but solaced herself with at least being able to still host a rehearsal dinner.

"It creates chaos otherwise," Melanie said quickly in that confident tone she took on when she spoke to her clients. Melanie's advice had been doled out for free for so long that the plan was to start offering wedding consulting services, but the spring rush had created so much business that they couldn't find a way to adjust to that idea just yet, or at least Chloe couldn't.

Abby walked over to a display of freesia and Sarah felt herself twitch. That definitely didn't fit the color scheme. If she started throwing purple into the mix then the bridesmaids' dresses would have to change too. And there was no time for that.

She gently guided Abby back to a beautiful arrangement of roses. Pink, peach, and white roses.

"I just figured people would gather at whatever table

they wanted to," Abby was saying. "It seems selfish of me to dictate where they will sit."

"No." Melanie shook her head firmly. "It will be a gift to them. I promise you. Do you want me to do the seating charts for you?"

Sarah knew that Chloe would have a fit if she heard Melanie offer this up, free of charge; the only loophole here was that Abby was marrying Melanie's brother, and of course, this could all be considered bridesmaid duties. But here and there Melanie would offer up advice that extended beyond the dress selling, veil selling, shoe selling nature, and Chloe's cheeks would go all red and her mouth would get all pinched and then she and Melanie would coexist in icy silence for the entire work day, leaving Sarah to rearrange the jewelry case a few dozen times with shaky hands. The way Chloe saw it, their responsibilities for the time being were to sell the merchandise.

"Well, before you take a look at the final guest list, I should tell you that there is going to be one new addition, actually," Abby said slowly. "A guy."

"Really?" Sarah grabbed her friend's arm. "Why didn't you tell me? Who is it? Is he cute?" But then of course she'd have Melanie to compete with. And Chloe too. And Chloe was so cool and chic and beautiful.

Abby swallowed. Hard. Her eyes drifted to Melanie. "It's...Doug."

Doug? Sarah looked at Melanie in horror. She had

gone completely still but her expression betrayed no emotion. Shock, Sarah thought. Total shock.

"How did this happen?" Melanie finally spoke. "Zach knows how much I hate him."

Hate? Love? Same thing, it would seem.

"You know that Jessica Paulson made the invitations. You know she's doing that stationary business now? When I handed her the invitation list, she asked if she could bring him as her plus one."Abby gave Melanie a look of apology. "I didn't know how to say no."

There had been rumors that the two were dating, and now, it would seem, that had been confirmed.

"You'll still come?" Sarah thought of last night, and how Melanie couldn't even be in the same bar as Doug.

"You have to!" Abby said, fear kicking her tone up a notch. "You're my bridesmaid! And…you're making my dress?" She crossed both sets of her fingers dramatically.

"Of course I'm making your dress," Melanie said, but she was frowning now, and Abby still looked a little pale, even if her eyes were gleaming at Melanie's decision. "And I'll come to the wedding. I have to. You're marrying my brother! But I'm bringing a date."

"Well, if you are then I am!" Sarah said, feeling her heart speed up in alarm. She didn't know who Melanie would find on such short notice any more than she would. Tim…Could she really do it?

Abby just smiled widely. "Wonderful. It's a plan then."

A plan, perhaps. But what was that saying about the best-laid plans?

Chapter Four

By ten o'clock on Monday, Jason had already treated a four-year-old with hives, a mother of three with a sore throat and a fear that it was contagious and would spread through the entire household, specifically to her husband, which would cause the world to "come to an end," and a sweet old woman who wouldn't stop batting her eyelashes at him.

Jason forced his attention to the chart in his hand. "It says here that you experienced a dizzy spell this morning."

"That's right," Mrs. Preston said, giving him a coy smile. "Though from the size of those biceps it looks like you wouldn't have any trouble catching me if I fell..."

Jason felt his eyes widen in surprise. Right. Time to get on with business. He set the clipboard on the counter and pulled his stethoscope into his ears. "Take a deep breath," he instructed.

"With pleasure." Mrs. Preston looked him deep into the eyes.

He didn't respond. Melanie would perhaps call that the lack of bedside manner, but he called it professionalism. If he fed into every patient's emotions, he would lose his objectivity. And something told him that humoring this woman would be the worst thing he could do. She was confused at best, but he had seen enough patients with similar symptoms that made him think there was more going on here.

"How old are you, Mrs. Preston?" he asked, as he stepped back from the table and wrote her stats on the chart.

"A lady never reveals her age," she said.

He gave a mild smile and leaned back on the counter. "True. But we'll let this fall under doctor-patient confidentiality."

"I'm twenty-nine," she said, blinking up at him.

He heaved a sigh. "Mrs. Preston, I'd like to refer you to St. Francis for some tests. Nothing to be too concerned about. Just a routine follow-up to make sure that we're fully aware of everything going on. You haven't bumped your head recently by any chance, have you?"

She held a hand to her head, her eyes taking on a worried look. "I don't think so. I don't remember."

"Well, I'd like to make a call and see if they can get you in today. Would you be able to get a ride to Shelter Port today?" It wasn't far, twenty-five, maybe thirty minutes at most, though an ambulance could get there much faster, but far enough that it would take a committed person to drive her there and back and sit with her while she had some tests done. He hoped that she hadn't driven herself to the office this morning. Last year in Boston he'd treated six people who were involved in an accident caused by a car going through a bakery window. The man responsible was driving without a license and had thought he was hitting the brakes, not the gas pedal.

"My granddaughter can drive me," she said. "She brought me here today."

A twenty-nine-year-old with a granddaughter, Jason thought. Now that was something you didn't see every day.

"Wonderful," he said. "I'll go to the lobby and speak with her while you dress."

"If you insist," she purred, and this time, despite himself and the standards he aspired to, Jason did laugh, but he quickly covered it with a cough.

"I'll be in the lobby, Mrs. Preston," he said, and God help him, she winked.

The lobby was small, but already full, and his father's receptionist, a woman by the name of Shelby who had taken over about five years ago when his mother had stepped back from the job to focus on charity work, was scheduling appointments. "How frequent is the vomiting? Both ends?" he heard her ask, and he muttered to himself. It was turning out to be a jam-packed day, but he didn't feel the rush he did back in the emergency room. Back in Boston, he was dealing with triage: gunshot wounds, catastrophic motor vehicle accidents, burn victims. Now he was dealing with ear infections and the common stomach bug. Time seemed to tick by, and his adrenaline wasn't pumping. He was hungry, and he was never hungry when he worked—he was too busy to think about food. But now he was eager for lunch. He knew he had an hour scheduled into his day between appointments.

"I'm looking for Mrs. Preston's granddaughter?" He looked around the room, surprised, but pleased, when he saw Sarah set down the celebrity magazine she was reading and walk over to him. He looked her up and down. "You're Esther's granddaughter?"

"That's right," she said smiling.

"Do you live with her?" he asked. He could only hope that his patient didn't live alone. Too many people like her did, and the consequences could be catastrophic.

"No, she lives at Serenity Hills. They have some nursing care on site, but they felt a doctor's visit was needed this time."

Serenity Hills was the retirement home out on the edge of town, a fine establishment, and one that his father paid frequent visits to over the years.

"When Melanie said you were a doctor, I didn't realize you'd be working here," Sarah said. "We're used to seeing—"

"My father?" He'd been getting that all day. A few people even questioned his credentials. Asked if he had graduated med school yet. He politely told them that he had. He was thirty years old and somehow, he was still perceived as the little boy with a bowl haircut who liked to listen to the heartbeats of the stuffed animals in the lobby.

He suppressed a sigh. This was small-town life. It would take some adjustment. And soon enough he'd be back in the city again.

"I'd like your grandmother to have some tests done. Can you take her to St. Francis today?"

"The shop opens late on Mondays, but I suppose I could ask Melanie if I can have the day off."

"Please do," he said, knowing that Melanie would accommodate the request.

Sarah frowned. "Is there something wrong with my grandmother?"

"I'll know more after the tests," he said. "She appears to be in good physical strength, but I think a neurological exam is needed."

"And you can't do that here?"

It was another drawback of small-town life. This was a clinic, with one doctor, one nurse, and one receptionist. Anything that required testing or a serious case had to be referred to one of the nearest hospitals. He felt helpless when he shook his head. "I'm afraid we're not equipped for that type of thing here. But I can refer you to a doctor there. I was in pre-med with him at University of Maine."

"Thanks, Jason," Sarah said, and then winced. "I mean, Doctor."

"Jason is fine," he smiled.

"First name basis, are we?" Mrs. Preston said as the nurse led her out to the lobby. Doreen's eyes were wide as they met Jason's. There was no telling what the patient had been telling her. "Sorry, Sarah, but I saw him first."

Sarah's cheeks turned the color of her bright pink shirt. "Grandma!" She looked up at Jason, apology in her big blue eyes. "I'm sorry."

"Letting him down easy, are you, my girl?" Mrs. Preston shook her head.

"No!"

"Not your type?" Mrs. Preston asked pertly.

"No!" Sarah glared at her grandmother and then looked desperately up at Jason. "I mean, that's not what I mean. It's not like that. I don't want you to think—I mean, it's not that I don't find you attractive. It's just—" She stopped talking, perhaps realizing that she was digging herself deeper, the color in her cheeks now hovering on something darker than pink, more into the red territory.

Jason wished she hadn't stopped. He was thoroughly amused, and flattered. Sarah was a pretty girl. He liked what he knew of her, too.

But that was the problem, wasn't it? He'd come across many women like Sarah over time. And every time he couldn't quite bring himself to take an extra step forward.

Melanie always scolded him, told him he worked too hard, that he was missing out, that there was more to life.

But Melanie didn't know the half of it. And at this point in his life, he wasn't sure that she ever would. And that was something he should have made peace with a long time ago...

*

Melanie hung up the phone and closed her eyes. Sarah needed the day off. Of course Melanie had said yes. Her grandmother needed tests done, at St. Francis, today. Jason had said so. And who was she to argue with that? Despite the way she jabbed him, she knew that Jason was an excellent doctor. It was his calling, who he was meant to be. She could still remember the time she'd fallen on some rocks near the beach and Jason had reached into his backpack and retrieved a first-aid kit, when he must have only been about ten. He'd cleaned and bandaged the cut, and he'd even called the next day to see how she was feeling. Her mother had thought that was adorable, of course, and told that story every time she saw him, which wasn't so often anymore.

Now, though, it seemed to her that Jason was in and out with patients in as little time as necessary. Sometimes she wondered if he even knew their names. He seemed stressed in their video chats, and, if she was being honest, not exactly happy.

Tired, she'd told herself. Of course he was tired, but

now she wondered if there was more to it. He didn't open up much about his life back in Boston, at least not outside of work. He mentioned a date if she pried, but there was never anyone special. She wondered if Jason was lonely, if work would be enough, if she should be the one giving him the pep talk rather than receiving one.

Well, there was no time for wondering about that today. With Sarah gone, that meant that she would have to face her cousin Chloe alone. Or save her conversation about the dress and her plans to expand the business for another day, a day when she had a buffer, a day when Sarah was at her side.

This was tempting. About as tempting as that pizza she had nearly ordered last night. (Extra cheese and sausage had been her staple for the last year, to the point where Ritchie DiSotto didn't need her to recite her order when she called, and she didn't need to ask the total. She knew it down to the penny, with a generous tip included.) But then she thought of the promise she had made to her friends. The promise she had made to herself. This year would be different.

Besides, if she kept eating all that pizza, how would she fit into her bridesmaid dress? It was already snug as it was. And now with the knowledge that Doug would be there…. Well, if that wasn't motivation, she didn't know what was.

A ripped seam was entirely possible at this point, she thought, as she bent down to select her shoes from the floor of her front closet and felt the button of her pants dig into her stomach. Yes, that was certainly motivating. The last thing she needed was to be the center of attention for all the wrong reasons. With any luck, she'd just fade into the distance, looking amazing, of course, while Doug did his thing from across the room.

Preferably that thing was writhing in extreme longing, but she'd take regret too. Really, Jessica was a nice enough girl, but what was so much more likeable about her? Was Doug really going to find what he was looking for with Jessica if he couldn't find it with her?

Come to think of it, Doug had never really expressed what he was looking for. He hadn't talked about the future, not unless you counted what he planned to eat for dinner or how he wanted to spend the weekend.

Chloe was already in the shop when Melanie turned the key at exactly noon. On Mondays the shop didn't open to the public until the afternoon, giving them a chance to catch up on paperwork or alterations in the morning hours without interruptions. And Mondays were meeting day. The benefit to working in a small space was that they were usually caught up on everything that was going on, but the chance to sit and discuss everything in a peaceful setting (or usually peaceful setting) was beneficial.

In all the years since they had decided to open the shop together, they had never missed a Monday meeting. It would be easy to slack off, given that they were family, easy to fall out of the habit, but they were professionals, and they were eager to be successful business owners.

They just didn't always see eye to eye on how to make that happen.

"I brought sandwiches!" she said, holding up the bag from Angie's. She was particularly proud of herself that when Leah had offered a complimentary chocolate chip cookie to go with the order, Melanie had summoned the self-control to decline it. Even when she was told it was still warm from the oven, she couldn't be swayed, though in fairness, she did hesitate. "Turkey on wheat for you and veggie for me."

"Veggie?" Chloe looked up from her spreadsheets and frowned at her. "You usually get that thing with brie."

"And I usually don't have to spend an evening with Doug either," she said simply.

Chloe's eyes were round. "It seems I missed a lot when I was gone," she said, motioning Melanie to the storage room which doubled as their back office space. "Don't tell me you're dating Doug again."

Dating Doug again? Did those sorts of things even happen? Not in her world. Sure, she'd seen other people in town reunite with old love interests, Zach and Abby being two of them, but those relationships had foundations, history. What she and Doug had was...fun, she supposed.

"Jessica invited him to the wedding. I assume they're dating." It was bound to happen, of course, that one of them would move on. She'd just hoped she would have been the first. How that was supposed to happen while she was eating her emotions in front of the television for the past year was questionable, though.

"Yikes." Chloe pushed her low ponytail off her shoulder and unwrapped her sandwich.

Melanie did the same with hers, sighing at the contents. She did love cheese. So much. Cheddar, gouda, a nice nutty gruyere. And that tomato and brie on a warm baguette from Angie's was something she looked forward to each day, true.

But she was staying strong! And she would remain strong all through this meeting. She glanced up at her cousin. Her stomach did a strange sort of flip. Chloe was always so put together, her clothes neat and pressed, her jewelry and makeup carefully thought out in a way that looked effortless. She never showed a hint of weakness or vulnerability. She was in charge. Of her life. Of this store. She wasn't easily swayed. Chloe was single, decidedly so, and while she dated over the years, she never would have slugged boxed wine and had to consider ordering maternity pants after wallowing for a year.

Chloe was, to some people, an ice queen. But they didn't know her like Melanie did. Chloe might be cool on the outside, but inside? Chloe was a mess. A hot one. Her mere anxiety over finally expanding this business was proof of that.

"How was the conference?" Melanie asked, hoping to ease her way into the conversation.

"Informative," Chloe said briskly. She set her

notebook in front of her. Her food remained on a napkin. There were several bridal industry events each year, and she and Chloe took turns attending them.

Melanie's pad of paper was already covered with crumbs. "Any new design trends I should know about?"

"We can talk about that later. I'm more interested in hearing what I've missed. Did Abby Harper's dress arrive?"

Melanie nodded. It was an easy question, but her heart rate was already speeding up. Soon, she would have to admit to what had gone wrong with Abby's dress. And then she would have to admit to what she had agreed to do for Abby. And then…She took a big bite of her sandwich. She really needed the brie on a day like this.

"We also got the catalogues for the new fall lines."

"Excellent." Chloe jotted something down on her notebook. Her handwriting hadn't changed since the third grade. It was still loopy, legible, and achingly symmetrical. "And everything went smoothly with Abby's dress? She had a fitting yesterday, I saw on the calendar."

Melanie gulped. "The dress didn't work out after all. There was a mistake with the order but she wasn't willing to have them redo it."

"Well, there wouldn't have been time anyway!" Chloe had stopped eating. Even though she wasn't a bridesmaid, Abby was a client, and Chloe took clients very seriously. "Did she finally agree on something we have in stock?"

"Not really," Melanie said slowly. She wrung her hands under the table. "She asked me to make her a custom dress."

"Oh, please!" Chloe scoffed, reaching for her sandwich again.

Melanie knew what she was thinking, that Abby was high-maintenance, overly picky, that she would never be satisfied. "I said I would do it."

There, it was out.

Chloe's jaw slacked. "Do you know how much time that will take?"

Oh, did she. Just the sketching alone had taken up the better part of her weekend. She was just thankful that Abby had agreed to her design last night, with a few minor tweaks. She'd placed the fabric order first thing this morning.

"It's a gift to her. And I enjoy doing it. And…" Say it, Melanie, just say it! "And I think that other brides would be interested in custom gowns, too."

Chloe was already shaking her head, chewing rapidly, crumbs now flying. Melanie pressed on. "We've talked about it before. And I worked on a lot of wedding dresses in design school." For as different as the cousins could be, they had both followed the same path. It had brought them together in this endeavor. But recently, it felt like it was driving them apart.

Chloe's face was now completely blank, but Melanie thought she could hear her breathing. Deeply.

"We can both sew. Remember all those clothes we used to make for our dolls when we were kids? And you didn't go to design school just to sell other people's dresses, Chloe!"

"I also didn't go to design school just to run my business into the ground."

"But why bury our talents?" Melanie's voice rose, and she was thankful for a moment that Sarah wasn't around to witness this. "We didn't open the shop just to keep it the same forever. And we've always talked about offering wedding consulting services. The brides are always asking our advice—"

"Which you give out, even though it's not your job." Chloe's mouth was set.

"They're asking my opinion! I'm happy to give it!" Melanie sat back in her chair. This was getting too heated already, just as she knew it would.

"Now isn't the time to expand the business. We have enough business to be turning a profit and enough business that we needed additional help."

"Exactly. We have Sarah now," Melanie pointed out. "She can handle the fittings. I thought we brought her on so that we would be free to expand things around here."

"And what about the walk-ins?" Chloe asked, and Melanie knew she had her there. The walk-in traffic could derail the most streamlined day. And much as it was tempting to change their business model to appointment only, they didn't want to turn off any new customers.

"Most of them are browsers," Melanie said. They both knew this. "Then I'll handle the fittings and Sarah can handle the walk-ins. I can plan my design work around the appointments."

"It's one thing to talk about offering wedding consulting. But now custom gowns, too? We can't be expanding in all these directions!"

Chloe was shaking her head, and Melanie felt a wave of frustration. It was this way any time she broached a new idea. Chloe was conservative. She was cautious. She liked to play things safe. And even though Melanie understood why, she hated that Chloe still let her past haunt her so much, and that it was impacting Melanie's plans too.

Melanie tried a new tactic. "I know that you have been wanting to do wedding consulting, Chloe. I think that's of high interest to you. You love going to these conferences and getting new ideas. Admit it. You'd love to put an entire concept together, not just a dress. You'd love to think about color schemes and all those little details that would make everything come together." If there was nothing Chloe didn't love, it was perfection. It calmed her.

Chloe wavered. "I can just see things getting backed up. This is our busy season, after all."

"But how will we know if we don't try?" Melanie asked.

"And what if we try and fail?" Ah, her cousin. Ever the optimist.

"Then we will know that we at least tried. Think of how exciting it would be to get back to doing what we really love and applying it to a business we are both already committed to."

Chloe set down her sandwich and blew out a breath. "How was it this weekend?"

"Pretty crazy," Melanie had to admit. On Saturday they'd had at least a dozen walk-ins, and after one woman tried on at least eight dresses, Melanie had discovered that she wasn't even engaged, much less in a relationship. That had frosted her, greatly, but what could she do? It wasn't the first time it had happened.

"As it is, we agreed not to take vacations during the busy seasons. Sometimes we both have to work the entire weekend, too, even though we had always tried to swap turns, and we hired Sarah to take that burden off us. And next Saturday we have to close early for the wedding since we're all invited. We'll lose business."

"It's a family wedding," Melanie said, but everything Chloe was saying was true. While they had always agreed to alternate weekends in the shop, it became unmanageable for one of them, and so a third person was brought in to alleviate the stress.

Chloe set her sandwich to the side. "I need to get some work done before my first appointment."

"I'd like to finish discussing this," Melanie said when Chloe pushed back her chair.

Chloe pulled open the door to the storefront. "And I'd like to get these weekend orders placed before we're delayed a day in shipment."

Melanie sighed and stuffed her sandwich back into the

bag, her appetite lost, which, considering her maternity pants were on their way back to the vendor, was probably a good thing.

Chapter Five

Sarah stopped over at Melanie's apartment that evening just as Melanie was dumping the contents of her boxed wine into the sink. Those days were over. As were the days of the bags of the processed cheese popcorn that she tossed into the bin. Doug had moved on first. Of course he had. Unless the pizza delivery guy was going to ask her on a date, and she would have had to decline that, considering he was fifty-two and married, she hadn't stood a chance all year, and she had no one to blame but herself.

"Oh!" Sarah's hand hovered over an unopened bag of potato chips where it rested in the trash can. "Do you mind?"

"Have at it," Melanie said. No use letting it go to waste, and now she regretted the purchase altogether. She usually stocked up, kept enough on hand for seven nights of pity parties and trash television, sometimes longer, so she could come straight home from work and not have to worry about going out or being seen. It had been comforting, at first, but then it became a habit, and one that never should have lasted as long as it had. Sure, once Sarah moved to town she found a friend to go out with, and that had somewhat broken the pattern, but not enough.

She surveyed the pantry with a critical eye, thinking of what she could keep and what she should really part with. The pretzels had been a favorite for a while, when she first started noticing the weight gain, and those she would still keep. "Take the tortilla chips and jar of fake cheese sauce while you're at it."

Sarah happily added all the items to a grocery bag she pulled from the pile that Melanie kept on hand. Melanie's mouth salivated only slightly as she handed over the jar. That cheese sauce may have been electric orange with a shelf life of a couple years, but oh, she could still taste it if she closed her eyes. Warm and spicy and…

Sarah was giving her a funny look. Perhaps the longing was showing in her face.

"You really sure you want to give all this up?" Sarah asked, extending the jar.

"I can always buy more," Melanie said, before she registered the thought. No! She would not be buying more. That would defeat the entire purpose of packing it up. "I want to stick to my diet this time. I've gotten into a rut this last year. I need to make some big changes. And I want to look good at Zach's wedding. You know my mother will be hanging those photos all around the house and they'll be there forever more. I don't want to cringe every time I see them."

"So it's not all about Doug being there, then?"

"Partly," Melanie admitted. "Is that terrible?"

"No," Sarah said matter-of-factly. "I'd probably be doing the same thing."

"Jessica Paulson!" Melanie clucked her tongue. She didn't have anything against Jessica; they had been classmates in school, of course, and they'd been on a field hockey team together one fall, both the worst players, usually benched, before realizing it wasn't for them. She supposed it wasn't who Doug had moved on with, but that he had. And that he had felt the need to reject her first.

"You were too good for him. He should regret what he did. But you shouldn't want him back either."

"I don't," Melanie said. And she didn't. Not really.

Sarah dug around in the pantry until she found a fresh bag of chocolate cookies. Melanie had forgotten about those. "I assume I can have these, too? Seeing as I have no ex to impress and Abby has confirmed that there are no eligible men coming to her wedding, I see no reason to deprive myself." Her smile faltered as she walked over to the small living room adjacent to the kitchen area and sank onto Melanie's favorite armchair.

Technically, it was a recliner. Another comfort splurge and one that really disturbed her brother. Zach claimed it reminded him of their grandfather's chair. It bothered him more than the boxed wine.

"Besides," Sarah said. "I have a bad feeling about my grandmother."

"Oh no!" Melanie closed the cabinet doors and gave her friend her full attention.

"It's nothing...physical. She's confused. She forgets things. It's just part of getting older, I guess. It could be worse. And I suppose I should be grateful to still have a living grandparent at my age."

Now Melanie felt like a first-class heel. She'd been so distracted by her meeting with Chloe that she hadn't even texted or called to check in on Sarah all day. She'd assumed no news was good news, but she should know best that sometimes when someone disappeared, they were hiding something they didn't want to have to talk about.

"Well, I have a business card in emotional eating as you know," Melanie said. "So I won't judge. But if you want to talk, I'm happy to listen."

"Thanks," Sarah said as she pulled open the bag of chips. "For now I think I'll stick with these, though."

"Fair enough." Melanie eyed the bag, her mouth watering. One little chip wouldn't make a difference, and with less than two weeks to go before the wedding, it wasn't like a miracle was going to happen or anything.

Still, she had her shape wear. She had a flattering bridesmaid dress thanks to Abby's excellent taste, when she ever actually committed to it. And she had a diet plan that would at least make her feel more confident.

"You want one, don't you?" Sarah's eyes gleamed, but Melanie just grabbed a half-eaten container of ice cream from the freezer and stuffed it in the garbage bag. Normally she would have enjoyed that straight from the carton with a spoon, maybe even some whipped cream sprayed directly on top.

Speaking of… She opened the fridge and grabbed the can from the inside door. It was light; she'd consumed most of the product. Into the garbage it went. Never again. Or only on special occasions. Occasions to celebrate. She was staying positive.

Man, it wasn't easy. Sometimes she marveled over how her cousin Chloe could stay so regimented. She would never admit it, but Melanie was positive she counted her calories. She still wore the same size she did back in high school. Melanie knew this because she had seen her wear her old cheerleading shirt on her way to the gym one day. Chloe went to the gym every morning before work. And after work, she jogged. Her apartment was so tidy that Melanie once asked her for a referral to her housecleaning service, and Chloe had laughed and said she didn't use a service, she did it herself.

Melanie was fairly certain that Chloe didn't sleep. Not much, anyway. How did she find the time?

"Of course I want some chips. I want all of it, not just

the chips, but the cookies and…" Oh, that cheese sauce. She shook her head. "But I want to feel good at that wedding more."

"And being a few pounds thinner will make you feel better? Or will having Doug live with regret make you feel better? Or…" Sarah frowned and set down the bag. "You don't want him back, do you?"

"Of course not!" Melanie scoffed, but she couldn't look at Sarah right now, at least, not in the eye.

"Melanie!"

"I know!" She closed her eyes and dropped the trash bag to the floor. "I know."

"He's bad news. He treated you terribly! You deserve better!"

"I know!" Of course she knew. She knew all these things. "But he's…he's so cute."

"Lots of men are cute," Sarah said. She gave a little shrug. "Jason is kind of cute."

Melanie felt her brow knit. Jason was decent looking, sure, but so was her brother. "It's not like that with me and Jason."

"Never?" Sarah seemed a little too curious for Melanie's comfort zone.

"No. Never." Well, that wasn't exactly true, was it? When she hadn't gotten a date for prom, Jason had stepped up to the plate and invited her himself. A pity date, she knew, but still, she'd had a good time, probably a better time than she would have had if one of the guys she'd been eyeing on the football team had asked her. He'd shown up with a corsage that matched her dress and he danced to all her favorite songs, and at the end of the night, a part of her wondered what would happen if he tried to kiss her?

"Your tone doesn't convince me." Sarah resumed eating the chips.

Melanie listened to her crunch. She felt her stomach rumble. "Maybe there was a time where I thought we might be a good match. He took me to prom. I was his pity date. And I will be again, if he's willing to be my plus one to the wedding."

"I figured you would ask Jason." Sarah said. "So you did once think you could be a match."

Melanie shook her head."I was young then. And besides, it's too late now."

"It's never too late!" Sarah said, her eyes popping. "How can you say that? Look at your own brother! Did you ever think that he and Abby would reunite and have a second chance?"

She thought about this for a moment. Zach had moved away, without Abby, a long time ago, leaving Abby angry and brokenhearted. Even when he'd returned to town, Melanie wasn't so sure that Abby would have him back, or where they each stood on their feelings. "No."

"But it happened! Where's your faith?"

Melanie stared into the contents of the junk food that had been her crutch for so long. "What can I say? I'm a little jaded when it comes to romance. It's not all about the dress and cake and carriage. And not everyone gets that far, either."

"Well, I intend to get that far," Sarah said firmly. "If the right guy ever crosses my path."

Melanie walked into the living room and dropped onto the couch. She was all too happy to switch the focus onto Sarah's love life instead of her own. "I think it's time to widen the pool. Maybe try online dating."

Sarah wrinkled her nose. "It just doesn't feel romantic."

"What do you want? To walk into a room and bump into a guy and look up and realize that your heart is beating wildly and you can't breathe or speak because you just know it's the one?"

"Yes!" Sarah exclaimed. "What's so wrong with that?"

"Nothing," Melanie said. "Sadly, I have the same fantasy myself." It was why she hadn't gotten out of her rut, she supposed. She hadn't wanted to try. She just wanted it to…happen.

"Maybe I'll give online dating a whirl," Sarah said with a sigh, sinking her hand deep into the bag of chips.

"Maybe I will too." Melanie said, even though her heart wasn't in it. After all, she needed a back-up plan if Jason didn't want to go as her date to the wedding.

But Jason wouldn't let her down, she knew. After all, he never had before.

*

Jason stayed at the office past the last appointment, looking over his father's notes, checking up on Esther Preston's test results. It was Alzheimer's, just as he'd feared, and he decided to talk to Sarah about it the next time he saw her, see if she had any questions the doctors at St. Francis hadn't been able to address.

Jojo's was up ahead, around the corner from the office. The outdoor tables had already been set up for the season, and Melanie was at a table near a heat lamp. Jason's mood lifted immediately, and for the first time all day, he was happy to be back in Oyster Bay.

"Hey," he said, as he pulled out a chair. "Am I late?"

She grinned. "I'm early. When are you ever late?"

He took a sip of water and glanced at the beer menu. "Are you accusing me of being too responsible?"

"I'm just saying that you're allowed to have a little fun once in a while." She gave him a knowing smile across the table and something in her eyes made his stomach tighten.

He cleared his throat, looked back at the menu. A drink was in order. A strong one.

"Anything new since we last spoke?" he asked, once they had ordered their drinks. When they were kids they talked every day, never running out of anything to say, but just as content to exist in companionable silence. Now that they both had careers and didn't live in the same city, those silences felt more awkward, and he didn't have as much of a handle of the day to day minutia that they once shared. He missed that, he realized now, feeling a sense of loss in his chest even though he was right here, talking to her now.

He supposed it was reality. He supposed it was inevitable.

"I officially agreed to make Abby's dress," she said with a dramatic shudder. "Chloe's not happy, but...I want this. And it feels good to want something."

He grinned, genuinely happy to see her so passionate about something again. "I couldn't agree more."

Her brow seemed to knit. "So, you're really happy in the emergency room? You think that's your calling?"

He loved his job, loved the fast pace and the thrill he felt when he pulled someone out of a bad situation. Loved the concept of being able to make a difference in someone's life. To save a life!

But he didn't always have those days. Sometimes a situation was hopeless, and those days, well, those days came with the job. The other days, the better days, those were the ones that kept you going, even if you were exhausted and lonely and living off juice and ramen and cold slices of pizza in the break room.

"Well, I've applied for a full-time job there," he replied. "My residency is almost over."

She nodded, a little sadly, which gave him a strange mix of feelings. He didn't want to let her down, but he also had to do what was best for him. And staying in Boston, pursuing the best possibility he could for his career, was just that.

"Sarah stopped by my place after work. She seemed a little down about her grandmother," Melanie said. "Is there anything I should do?"

"Send her to my office if she wants to talk things through," Jason said, and Melanie cocked an eyebrow. A small smile played at her mouth. "What?" he frowned, not knowing what she was getting at by her expression. Once, he could read her completely, but they didn't spend as much time together anymore, and she'd grown, evolved.

But she was still the same in many ways. Still thoughtful. Still kind. Still beautiful.

Nothing had changed. And that was both a good thing and a bad thing, he thought.

"You just called your father's office your office," she said pointedly.

Crap. He had, hadn't he? "Slip of the tongue. You know what I mean."

"Do I?" She tilted her head. "For as long as I've known you, you wanted to become a doctor because of your father."

"True," he said, though it was easy to lose sight of that sometimes. Once, medicine had felt noble and heroic. Lately it felt grueling and tiring and sometimes downright unrewarding. Objectively he knew that he was making a difference, though. Hell, he was saving lives! "But I'm not my father. And I don't want to follow in his path. But try telling my mother that."

"Oh, she just loves you and misses you. She's not the only one." Melanie waggled her eyebrows and Jason pushed back the uneasy feeling that stirred in his gut.

"My dad is acting weird too," Jason said, now that he thought about it. He spent a lot of time watching television and normally he didn't prioritize that. When he was home at night, he preferred to read. And he hadn't shown any anxiety over his patients or what he was missing in the office. He'd just handed Jason the key and caught him up on the histories of a few patients who had appointments this week.

"He just had a heart attack! Of course he's not himself."

"No," Jason said, shaking his head. "There's more going on here. He seems far too content not being at work. Relaxed, almost. It's not like him."

"Well, I think he trusts you to handle it in his absence," Melanie assured him.

Jason couldn't argue with that. "They want me to move back. At least, my mom does. Every time I turn around my mother has a new idea to tempt me into staying. This morning she offered to fix up my old bedroom, like I'm twelve or something. I had to remind her that I'm leaving a week from Sunday. Do you know how uncomfortable that bunk bed is?"

Melanie laughed. "Staying there is a challenge, I'm sure."

That was an understatement. This morning his mother

had also frowned at him for running out the door without a tie, saying even a small-town doctor was expected to dress the part. She didn't calm down until she saw the tie he had in his bag, a backpack that she then turned her attention on, saying that she would buy him a nice leather briefcase, today. Brown, like his father's.

"Seriously, this dinner was my saving grace. Tomorrow night she has bridge club so she'll be out, but the next night..." He could only imagine. "It's only Monday and I'm already dreading Wednesday. She told me she's making roast beef. You know what that means."

"Your favorite meal," Melanie said with a knowing shake of her head, and Jason felt his anxiety loosen. Melanie was the only other person in the world who knew what his favorite meal was.

"If she makes Yorkshire pudding then I'll know it's going to be a bad night," Jason said, and Melanie laughed. "Seriously, Mel, she won't stop asking me when my residency is over. I don't have the heart to tell her that I've applied to stay on there."

"Do you want me to come to dinner on Wednesday?" Melanie asked.

More than she knew. "Thank you. Yes. I owe you."

"Well," she said a little coyly. "Then maybe you could repay the favor, so to speak. You know that Zach is getting married a week from Saturday. And yes, I know that you RSVPd no back when the invitations went out."

"I didn't think I could get away then," he cut in. Of course he would have loved to have been there. Zach was like family. He'd probably eaten as many dinners with the Dillons over the course of his childhood as he had with his own parents.

"So I thought you could go as my date." She looked up at him from the hood of her lashes and something within him stirred.

"Your date?" He could barely suppress his smile.

"You know, pose as my date. It wouldn't be the first time. Remember prom?"

How could he forget prom? She'd been without a date, heartbroken, and he saw an opportunity to make both of them happy with one fell swoop. He'd asked her himself, thrilled when she'd said yes, even though there was a weight in his chest every time he considered that he was just the pity date.

"I was your pity date," she reminded him now.

No, he thought. Other way around. He hadn't been her first choice. But her…She'd always been his.

"Doug is going," she said, giving him a knowing look. "With Jessica Paulson. Remember her from school? Nice enough, but it obviously stings. Everyone knows that you and I are just friends, but there's nothing wrong with letting Doug think something more might be going on."

Just friends.

He'd been stuck in the friend zone since they were kids and somehow had never been able to break out of it.

Jason felt his back teeth graze. He really needed that beer. "Of course not," he said tightly.

"And of course I want you there for your excellent company! Who else would I want to spend the evening with?"

He swallowed back the disappointment and opened his menu. "No problem. I think I have a suit somewhere in my closet."

"You're the best!" Melanie said, leaning over the table to give him a rather awkward hug. She smelled like berries and vanilla with a hint of something flowery. She smelled liked Mel. She smelled like home.

He was the best, he knew it. But somehow, he was still not good enough.

Chapter Six

The Sawyer family house was only six doors down from Melanie's own parents' house, a yellow cape with black shutters that they'd lived in all her life. She stopped there on her way to dinner Wednesday night to drop off the dress her mother had selected to the wear for the wedding: a navy sheath in raw silk with a bolero jacket to cover the upper arms that Melanie's mother was always fretting about, even though her arms were probably in better shape than Melanie's right about now.

Melanie hadn't even made it to the front door when it flung open, shaking the boxwood wreath that hung from a metal hook.

"I thought I saw your car pull up!" Melanie's mother's eyes were bright as she eyed her carefully.

Melanie suppressed a sigh. She hated the scrutiny but

she loved the source. Her mother had been worried about her ever since Doug's departure. She was forever suggesting local clubs and events that Melanie should be a part of as a way of getting out of her rut. The latest being—

"I was just going to call you today to remind you about the new knitting classes going on at Beads and Bobbles. You know that Kelly Donovan is running them."

"Kelly Myers," Melanie corrected her as she stepped into her childhood home. Even though she hadn't lived there since graduating from high school, it still smelled the same, and even though she stopped by at least once a week for dinner or an errand or just to say hello, she still never failed to feel put at ease when she came inside. "Kelly is Hannah and Evie's half-sister. They don't have the same last name."

"Well, those classes have been filling up since she started running them in January," Karen said, closing the door. "I heard there are two spots available if we sign up today."

This was what her life had come to. While other women her age were shopping for wedding gowns or baby strollers or a starter home, she was spending her free time with her mother doing crafts. Maybe she could rope Sarah into signing up, too. If there was a third slot.

"When are the classes?" she asked, and she almost smiled at the delight in her mother's expression. Normally she just turned her down flatly, but she was feeling better these days, and more up for getting out and trying new things.

"This session starts tomorrow."

Melanie shook her head. That was way too close to the wedding. "I can't do this session. I have too much going on after work."

Her mother's eyes were round with surprise. "Well, that's okay. So long as you're keeping busy!"

Jesus, had her situation really been that pathetic? Sadly, she knew that it had been.

Just to set her straight in case her mother thought she was busy with dates or something of the romantic nature, she said, "Actually, I've been asked to make Abby's wedding dress."

Her mother blinked in confusion, and Melanie could tell that she couldn't decide whether to be disappointed or pleased. After all, Melanie was finally pursuing her love for design again, something that she'd shelved for too long. But it was an activity done in solitude, and Melanie knew how her mother felt about that. It made her twitchy and concerned and it made her suggest things like knitting classes to get her out of the house.

"Chloe was okay with this?" she asked cautiously, as Melanie walked into the dining room and set the dress box on the table. Her grandmother's china was in the buffet hutch and she smiled at the hand-painted pattern of colorful flowers and butterflies. Her mother had promised it would be hers someday (meaning when she got married) and she was relieved to see that she was sticking to her word and not giving it to Zach and Abby instead.

"Not exactly." Melanie rubbed her forehead. She didn't want to think about Chloe now. Ever since their conversation on Monday, Chloe had refused to even mention Abby's dress. "Anyway," she said, giving her mother a grin. "Your dress is ready. Do you want to try it on again?"

They'd already done the alterations and Melanie knew that it should fit fine, but she also knew that her mother didn't want to take any risks where this wedding was concerned.

"I'll try it on tonight and let you know if there are any adjustments needed. I have a sauce going on the stove that needs stirring. You're welcome to stay."

"I have dinner plans," Melanie said, and her mother's eyes lit up again.

"You and Sarah doing something fun?" Karen opened the box and stroked the dress, but it was clear that her wedding attire was the farthest thing from her mind right now.

"I think Sarah's doing something with her grandmother tonight," Melanie said.

She could see the burning question in her mother's eyes, the need to know, the strength to refrain, the hope that she was afraid to feel.

Sometimes Melanie didn't know if she wanted to finally find a guy to end her loneliness or to please her mother.

"Oh, I see." Karen tried to distract herself by lifting up the dress, but Melanie could see her mind spinning. "Have you thought about bringing anyone to the wedding?"

Yep. There it was. Melanie knew it was coming. One idea led to the next, and the seed had been planted that Melanie had a date tonight. She hated the thought of letting her down almost as much she hated the way it made her feel that her mother was so determined to see her settled down. Would the hints keep going until she had a ring on her finger? She didn't think she could bear it anymore than she could stand the constant feeling that her single status was some kind of disappointment.

"Jason's coming with me."

And there it was. Karen's face was the picture of joy. Her eyes shone and her smile was so broad that Melanie felt a kick of resentment. She hadn't smiled this much over Melanie's mention of making Abby's dress. Was having a boyfriend or the prospect of one the only thing her mother wanted for her?

"Jason is coming with you? How nice! I heard he was back in town. Is he still handsome? He always was a little cutie. Smart, too."

Melanie gave her mother a wry look. It was time to shut this down, and quickly. "Don't even go there. Jason and I are just friends."

And of course he was still handsome. It wasn't like he suddenly grew a new face. Jason was a good-looking guy, not that she was going to confirm such a thing to her mother. She'd just misread that comment entirely.

Still, the hope didn't completely leave her mother's face. "How is his father doing? I heard that he's improving quickly."

"I'll ask tonight. That's where I'm going for dinner." Crap. She probably should have kept that bit of information to herself. She certainly wasn't helping her case.

"I see!" Karen was doing a poor job of hiding her smile.

Melanie checked her watch, stifling a sigh. She should get going soon, and judging by the way this conversation was going, it wasn't soon enough.

"So you two are spending quite a bit of time together," her mother remarked.

Melanie picked up her handbag. It was officially time to leave. "Of course we're spending time together. He's like, my best friend."

"But it's been years since the two of you have spent real time together. Now you're both in your thirties."

"Gee, thanks for the reminder." Melanie rolled her eyes as she walked toward the front door. Thirty and single was a horrifying concept to her mother, who had been married at age twenty-two to her college sweetheart. To Karen, Melanie was nearing the point of spinsterhood.

"I'm just saying, sometimes things evolve."

"And sometimes things are perfect just as they are." Melanie turned and gave her mother a peck on the cheek.

The disappointment in the sigh she heard wasn't lost on her.

Her mother's intentions were in the right place, she told herself as she walked back to her car, but her ideas were truly ridiculous.

*

Jason had to keep himself from staring out the window until Melanie's car pulled into the driveway. It was an old habit, one he'd developed long before they'd turned sixteen and gotten their licenses. Before then, he would look for a pretty girl on a bike, the anticipation always fresh, even though seeing Melanie was a regular occurrence.

Today, though, he had extra reason to wish she would hurry up already. His mother had been asking about the clinic since the moment he had walked in the door, before he could even drop his bag or go into the den to check on his dad, who was spending his recovery on his favorite recliner in front of the new flat screen television that filled a good portion of the opposite wall. The medical journals that he had always subscribed to sat on the coffee table, untouched. It was disturbing, and it made Jason uneasy.

"It's a busy job for one person to run that clinic, as I'm sure you can see," she said now, as she opened the oven to check on the roast.

Jason did see, but he always had. People always got

sick, but what happened when the only doctor in town did? Driving all the way to St. Francis wasn't practical on a regular basis, and not every ailment required an emergency room visit either.

"He should have brought another doctor on staff years ago," Jason said, but even as he said it, he knew what his mother meant by her statement, and he also knew that nothing he could say would stop her from eventually coming out with it.

"Well, with you in med school, he didn't want to be disloyal." She didn't look at him as she closed the oven door and set the timer again. "He didn't know what your plans would be."

"Are you saying that I was being disloyal by staying in Boston?" He knew he shouldn't have said anything. He should have made an excuse, gone into the den, watched a few minutes of the game. Melanie would be here soon enough. But he couldn't hold it in anymore. And he hated the guilt that was creeping higher and higher with each hour that he was back in Oyster Bay.

It had been bad enough when he'd gotten the call about his father, knowing he couldn't jump in the car and rush straight home. They were short staffed as it was—one doctor was on a honeymoon and the other still hadn't returned from maternity leave. But he was here now. As soon as he could be. It wasn't good enough, he knew it, but it was the best he could do.

"Your father is proud of the work you've done at the hospital," was all his mother said. She began mashing the potatoes. Usually they were his favorite part of the meal. Now he really wished that she hadn't insisted on cooking him something he loved. It made the thought of announcing that he hoped to take a permanent position in Boston all the more painful.

"Well, I hope that Dad will consider bringing on an extra set of hands now," Jason said.

"Couldn't agree more," Irene said. "It's too much for one man. What happened is proof."

"What happened last week was the result of a poor diet," he told his mother. They both knew how much his father loved his soft cheeses and fried snacks.

"He's always on the go! One of the reasons I left the clinic was because I hoped it would encourage him to see that there is more to life than just his practice. I'm always telling him to slow down. But now I'm going to insist on it," she said firmly.

Jason frowned, not liking the certainty in her tone, and unsure of what she was implying. Fortunately, before he could ask, the doorbell rang. "That will be Melanie," he said, the relief evident in his voice.

It took everything in him not to scoop her in for a hug when he opened the door and saw her standing there in a white blouse and pink skirt, a bouquet of purple flowers in her hand.

But then, it always took him a lot not to scoop her in for a hug. Not to touch her. Not to cross a line that was invisibly drawn years ago, when they were still just kids.

"What took you so long?" he asked instead in a low voice, because no doubt his mother was listening from around the corner. She'd always hoped that something would develop between him and Melanie. He didn't have the heart to tell her that that made two of them.

She rolled her eyes. "You don't want to know."

They shared a little smile as she slid past him into the hallway and made her way to the back of the house where his mother wasted no time in greeting her with a hug. "It's been too long! And flowers! My, how thoughtful. I'll get these in a vase."

"How's Dr. Sawyer?" Melanie asked, looking around.

"He's relaxing in the den. Still tired, of course." Irene glanced in Jason's direction.

He felt his shoulders stiffen. "Can I get you a drink, Mel? Wine?"

"White wine would be great," she said.

He grabbed a beer for himself. Back in Boston he never had a beer before dinner, or with dinner for that matter. But back in Boston he was always on call, most of the time sitting around the hospital break room, often too tired to even bother with dinner. He had to admit that it was sort of nice to clock out at the end of the day, to have a routine. But it wasn't so nice to know that tomorrow he would see a few cases of the common cold, maybe a sprained wrist. He knew it suited his father, but Jason had always wanted something more.

He glanced at Melanie as he handed her a glass of wine. He'd always wanted a lot more, hadn't he?

*

Jason hadn't been exaggerating when he said that his mother was laying it on thick. Melanie struggled to look him in the eye, and she had to hurry up and drink from her water glass every time he poked her leg under the table.

"It's wonderful to see you looking so healthy, Dr. Sawyer," Melanie said as she took a bite of the Yorkshire pudding. Yep, Jason was in trouble, all right. It was more than obvious that Irene didn't just want him to come back to Oyster Bay, but also to work at the family practice.

"A little rest does wonders," Irene commented, nodding firmly. "He's worked too hard for too long without any back-up. I can't even remember the last time we had a vacation."

There was a jab at her left knee. Melanie kept her eyes firmly on her plate.

"It's not always easy to own a business," Melanie agreed. "Chloe and I were just discussing how difficult it is for us to get away from the shop, and we have each other."

She glanced at Jason, feeling his glare, and realized she had misspoken. Flustered, she opened her mouth to correct herself, but her comment seemed to be lost already. Irene had a one-track mind, and she wasn't concerned with the status of Bayside Brides.

"It's very difficult to own your own business," she

said, her eyes never straying from Jason. "But so rewarding."

"Mom, Zach's getting married next week," Jason blurted.

She gave him a strange look. "Of course. We were invited. You were too, as I recall."

"And now he's coming!" Melanie smiled. "He's my plus one."

"Abby filled in as a receptionist for Shelby a while back, when Shelby had to leave town to take care of her mother." Dr. Sawyer smiled. "Nice girl, that Abby."

"You're going together?" Irene's eyes darted from her son's to Melanie's and then flicked over to her husband, who didn't seem to read anything into this statement.

Melanie again had the distinct impression that she had said something wrong. "The food was lovely, Mrs. Sawyer." She set her fork down on the edge of her plate. It was probably time to go soon.

"Well, I do what I can for Jason." Irene gave her son a long, lingering stare, and Jason's eyes popped with a plea for Melanie's help.

"Can I help you clear the dishes?" she suggested.

Irene pushed back her chair. "Thank you, Melanie. You've always been such a sweet, helpful girl." She gave another long, hard stare at her son as she gathered up two place settings and disappeared into the kitchen.

Melanie heard Jason heave a sigh as she passed him and walked into the kitchen. Irene was pulling dessert plates from the cabinet. A pie sat on the counter, waiting to be sliced.

"Thank you, Melanie," she said, when Melanie started rinsing the dishes in the sink. "We've missed seeing you around here."

"And I've missed being here," she admitted. After all, as a child, she knew every inch of this house nearly as well as her own. She and Jason used to play hide and seek in the basement, and build forts out of the living room couch cushions.

"We're hoping that with Jason's residency ending soon he will finally come back to town for good." Irene looked at her carefully as she set a pie cutter on the counter, as if gauging what Melanie might know.

Melanie focused on the dishes. "That would sure be nice." And it would be. But she also knew that it would never happen.

"He's always had a soft spot for you," Irene continued, giving a wistful smile.

It was a strange thing to say, and Melanie didn't quite know what she meant. Deciding not to ask, she said instead, "Well, he's always been a wonderful friend to me. The best, really."

"Friends? Is that what you young people call it these days?" Irene shrugged and lifted the pie and Melanie took that as her cue to take the dessert plates and four forks. Yep, it was definitely time to leave soon.

The air in the dining room was heavy when they entered despite the cool spring evening that they could see out the two large windows that faced the front yard. Melanie sat down at the table, and Jason immediately dug into his pie. Half a slice went into his mouth at once. She wasn't quite sure that he'd manage to get it down.

"I forgot the ice cream!" Irene exclaimed suddenly.

Jason held up a hand. "It's delicious just as it is, Mom. Really."

Melanie nodded. "Really, Mrs. Sawyer. It's delicious." Following Jason's cue, she took as large of a bite as she could manage, barely able to smile and hold it all in at the same time.

"I should get the ice cream," Irene said, pushing her chair back.

"It's fine, Mom, really. Besides, Melanie and I need to go into town tonight. I still need a gift for the wedding."

Another kick under the table. Melanie swallowed down her food. "Oh. Yes. Me too!"

Irene shrugged and went back to her own slice of pie, and as quickly as they both could without being rude, Jason and Melanie finished their plates, bid their goodbyes, and left out the front door.

Melanie could finally start laughing when they were on the cool front lawn, a warm, salty breeze blowing in from the ocean a couple miles away. "That reminds me of the time you signed us up for the pie-eating contest at the summer festival," she said, smiling at the memory. They were both so competitive, even back then, and she didn't even know what the prize was, at least not anymore. She just knew that she intended to win.

"I won every time I signed up," Jason said with a devilish grin. "You only lasted that one year."

"I'm not accustomed to shoveling food in my face," she remarked as they walked to her car, which was where she assumed they were going, because going back inside didn't seem to be an option.

"I'm not either," he said, as he slid into a passenger seat.

"Where are we going?" she asked as she stuck her key in the ignition. After all, her gift for Abby and Zach had been purchased months ago: some new, high-tech kitchen gadget that Abby would put to use.

"To the pharmacy. I think I have heartburn from eating so fast." His face was twisted in pain.

"It's pretty obvious that your mom is hoping to convince you to stay in town," she said as she backed out of the driveway.

"She's not going to be the one to convince me of that," he said, looking out the window.

Melanie frowned, thinking that was a strange way of wording things. "But someone could convince you to stay?"

He glanced at her sidelong and then back out the window. "It's a nice night," he said. "Want to grab a nightcap after we get those antacids?"

"Is that something you would recommend to your patients, Doc?" Melanie laughed.

"Probably not, but I'm an exception to the rules." He

grinned and something in her heart went all warm and soft.

He had that right. Jason had always been an exception to every rule. He was smart, sweet, caring, handsome, and completely devoted to her. And she could be herself around him without having to worry about things like how her hair looked or if her makeup was perfectly applied.

If only more guys could be like Jason, she thought with a sigh.

Chapter Seven

The next morning brought rain, and with rain came twitchy brides. Abby had a back-up plan, as most of the brides did, usually involving tents that were on hold just in case they were required, but it didn't stop them from worrying about beautiful white shoes and dress trains dipping into puddles as they dashed from the car to the ceremony.

Seeing as Melanie wasn't getting married anytime soon, she liked the rain: it gave her an excuse to be inside. It slowed the pace, and it helped her to concentrate and relax: two things that seemed to be at odds these days.

"Enjoy the shoes," she said to the excited bride as she handed over the bag, secured with a light blue ribbon, the shop's signature color. This particular customer planned to wear her mother's wedding gown but she was buying all her accessories through Bayside Brides. "Now you have your something new."

"And my something old and borrowed. And my something blue," she said, motioning to the ribbon that was tied around the shoebox. The color had been painstakingly chosen (Chloe must have rejected at least one hundred perfectly good shades for being too dark, too light, too green, too purple) and used throughout the store, from the paint on the walls to the ribbons that they used to box each product. Melanie had to admit that Chloe had chosen well. She was a master with color, and she had an eye for the smallest detail, which was why she would be the best consultant of the three of them, if she would ever agree to expand their scope.

The bride hesitated at the counter. "I was wondering, though, about maybe embellishing the dress a bit. It's all satin, but rather plain, and well, it is pretty old fashioned. Do you do custom work here?"

This was just the kind of project that Melanie would love to take on, but she saw Chloe stop fluffing veils across the room.

"We might be doing that at some point in the future," Melanie said, forcing her eyes back on the client. After all, this woman's wedding wasn't for another eight months. A Christmas wedding. She had only purchased the shoes so early because they were part of a winter clearance sale and happened to be exactly what she had in mind: satin, kitten heel, classic. They were a perfect complement to the dress she'd shown pictures of, and Melanie knew in her heart that the dress did need just a bit of bling to complete the vision.

"Wonderful!" The bride beamed as she left the store, the wedding bells jingling as the door opened and then closed.

Chloe wasted no time in approaching the counter. There was still one other customer in the store, but she was clearly just browsing near the tiaras. "Why would you say that to her? We have an agreement."

"No," Melanie said. "We have a disagreement." She walked around the counter to the shoe rack to straighten the other pairs and box up the styles that hadn't made the cut.

Chloe was quick at her heels, her voice low but insistent. "Custom work takes time. It's a lot of back and forth with the client."

Melanie smiled at the woman who waved as she left the store. Yep, just a browser. Melanie had learned early on that if an engagement ring wasn't spotted, then the women were likely just admirers. Or dreamers.

"We already deal with that," Melanie pointed out. She struggled to get two stilettos back in their box and then realized it was because she'd picked up the wrong one. "But think of how rewarding it would be. You love seeing an entire concept through from start to finish. I know it makes you crazy when someone doesn't pull everything together the way you so expertly could."

Flattery, it usually worked. But not with Chloe.

She folded her arms over her chest. "We'd have to charge more, and then we might lose clients."

"Clients who don't want something custom have the option of buying off the rack!" Honestly, Melanie didn't see why Chloe was so determined to shoot her idea down, but then, Chloe had always been risk adverse. It was a miracle she ever dared to have her own business at all, in some ways. But then, she supposed that Chloe viewed it as job security. "It's no different than with the jewelry. Some people buy what we have in stock. Some people commission Beth to make them something more special and unique."

Beth Sanders technically ran the craft store, but more and more she was taking orders for one-of-a-kind statement necklaces for the clients at Bayside Brides, and Melanie wondered how long it would be before Kelly Myers took over Beads and Bobbles and moved that store in her own direction. Beth's jewelry sold so well that they'd recently formed a partnership, ordering ten pieces a week from her that they kept in a special case near the other costume sets, and Beth sold items in her own store as well, things that weren't as appropriate for brides and more for the everyday customer.

She dropped off new inventory every Thursday, in preparation for the weekend rush. Come to think of it, she'd be stopping by any minute, a saving grace perhaps, considering Sarah was on lunch break and Chloe clearly not happy, but Melanie wasn't ready to be interrupted just yet.

"Just think about it," Melanie said to her cousin as she tucked the last shoebox in place. "Please?"

Chloe hesitated. "Fine."

Satisfied that she had gotten as far as she had with that conversation, Melanie checked the appointment book while Chloe grabbed her handbag and left for lunch. Her stomach growled and she would have loved nothing more than to dash over to Angie's for a nice cheesy sandwich. The thought of the can of low-sodium soup she'd packed to heat up was so uninspiring. Still, she was on a mission. She was moving forward. And damn, if it didn't feel good.

With no other appointments on her schedule until two, she decided to use the time to work on Abby's gown. She already had all of Abby's measurements from her fitting for the dress that hadn't come to be, and with those in hand she wanted to finish the pattern today. The fabric had arrived; she'd received a call from the post office this morning. She'd pick it up on her own, once Chloe returned. She hadn't dared let it come right to the store, lest Chloe run interference or it start another argument. The shop had a few other orders on wait, anyway. The latest shipment of veils from their supplier had come in just in time, as they were down to only two, and both were short. Several brides preferred something a bit longer.

She was so immersed in creating the pattern that she didn't even remember her soup, or hear the storage room door open.

"There you are!" Beth grinned as she stepped inside the room and looked at the paper spread out on the large work table. "Is this for Abby's dress?"

"She told you?" Word certainly traveled fast in Oyster Bay. With that in mind, she supposed it was good she hadn't tried to keep this little project from Chloe.

"Kelly did," Beth said, which of course made sense. Now that Kelly was on staff at Beads and Bobbles, she and Beth had grown close. With Kelly's half-sisters being Abby's cousins, she supposed that by some extension Kelly was going to be family come the wedding day, too. "She's hoping to commission her own custom gown if Noah pops the question."

Melanie set down her pencil. Noah Branson and Kelly had been dating since Christmas. "They're already that serious?"

"I don't think they're at that point yet, but if you ask me, he's the one."

The one. Of course he was the one. Kelly had come to town for the holidays and fallen in love and stayed here, made a life here.

"Wouldn't it be amazing to find the one?" She sighed as she studied her pattern again. "Someone to complete your sentences, someone who knows just what you're feeling without you having to say anything, someone who can finish your thoughts. Someone who will make you laugh. Someone who is always there."

Putting it that way, she supposed that person was

already in her life. But then Jason was different. She didn't think of him that way.

She paused. No. Definitely not.

Besides, all too soon Jason would be gone again. He'd made that clear, over and over. And this time, there was no hope of him coming back. It wasn't just med school or a residency program anymore. Jason had made his choice. And he'd chosen city life.

Her heart felt a little heavy as she tackled the neckline of the pattern. No sweetheart neckline for Abby! And she had better not have a change of heart about that.

"Right now my one and only is my cat, and I'm not afraid to admit that. But I probably should be." Beth laughed and pushed her long braid of hair off her shoulder. "Well, I have to get back to the shop. Want me to leave this week's items on the counter out front?"

"That would be great," Melanie said. She watched wistfully as Beth went back into the storefront, leaving the door ajar. Beth may not have found the one just yet, but she was pursuing her passion, not hiding it anymore, and that was more than Melanie could say for herself.

Well, until now, she thought, studying her pattern with a critical eye.

The bells jangled in the storefront, no doubt Beth leaving. A few minutes another jangle of bells, and this time it was probably Sarah returning from lunch. It was rainy and damp and it was a Thursday at noon. The chances of a walk-in were slim, and she was eager to trace out the entire pattern before her lunch break ended and her afternoon filled with fittings. Another jangle of bells. Chloe. Her breaks were often short. Melanie's heart rate sped up as she worked to reach a stopping point, but it was no use, the door opened and there was her cousin, her face red, her eyes steely.

"Are you working on Abby's dress pattern?" she asked.

"It's my lunch break," Melanie reminded her, not even disguising her impatience. They were partners, fifty-fifty, and she didn't appreciate being bossed around.

"Well, there are two customers out front and I walked into an empty store. It's a good thing that I forgot my cell phone and came back or who knows what would have happened while I was gone."

Now it was Melanie's turn to go red. She swallowed hard. It wasn't like her to slip up, and Chloe knew it.

"I'm sorry. It won't happen again." She folded up the pattern and tucked it into her bag that was hanging by a hook near the microwave. So much for her soup.

"This is why I don't want to expand," Chloe said. "Can't you see? We are only two people. Three with Sarah. But we're already busy enough."

Melanie squared her shoulders and pushed through the door into the storefront, wearing her best customer service smile. She didn't see what Chloe meant. Not at all. Yes, she had messed up, gotten distracted, not been as attentive as she usually was, but as for not expanding the business…

That just required a little imagination—something Chloe had lost along the way. Jason had helped her rediscover hers. The least she could do was pay it forward.

*

"I hear that Chloe really let you have it today," Sarah said as Melanie turned the key in the brass lock of the shop door. She'd come in at the tail end of the conversation, and danced around the feuding cousins all afternoon. "Why is she so reluctant to expand the business? I thought that's why you brought me in, so you could get into wedding consulting services."

"It was why we brought you in," Melanie confirmed. She shook her head as she lifted the canvas bag holding supplies for Abby's dress onto her shoulder. "Spring is always a crazy time of year. Chloe will calm down soon. I hope."

"Anything I can do to help?" Sarah offered. After all, she'd love to do more than button up the backside of gowns. When she was hired, she was looking forward to working on the consulting side of things eventually. "You do know that I subscribe to six different bridal magazines and have since college."

"You probably shouldn't reveal that on a first date." Melanie laughed. "Or any date."

"What date?" Sarah sidestepped a puddle. She had left her rain boots in the storage room but didn't want to go back. The clouds had parted and the forecast called for blue skies tomorrow into the weekend. "There's a speed dating event at that fondue place we went to for Valentine's Day. This Saturday night. Want to go?"

Melanie seemed to cringe, just as Sarah knew she would. "I might have plans with Jason…"

Sarah smiled to herself. She knew that Melanie would make an excuse like that which was why she was prepared. "He's coming too. I already asked him."

Now she had Melanie's full attention. Her eyes were wide as she stood at the crosswalk, and she didn't even seem to notice that they had a walk sign. "You asked him to go?"

Sarah nodded happily. "I had to stop in to his office on my lunch break to pick up some prescriptions for my grandmother. I mentioned it and he agreed." Of course there was no sense in mentioning that before he had agreed to come he had asked if Melanie was going and she had jumped the gun and said yes.

It was interesting, she thought now, trying to read Melanie's expression. At first she'd assumed they were each using the other as an excuse to get out of something. Now she wondered if there was more going on that they weren't revealing to her…or even to each other.

"Why would Jason be interested in finding a potential match in Maine?" Melanie asked. Her cheeks were getting a little blotchy.

Sarah shrugged. "Beats me. Maybe he's just looking to have a little fun. Flirt. Unwind. See if love will strike! Or maybe he's thinking of staying."

Melanie's jaw was set. She turned back to the crosswalk. They'd missed their chance, but the traffic was light, and they decided to make a run for it.

"So you'll come?" Sarah asked when they reached the other side of the street.

"I really should spend the time working on Abby's dress," Melanie said. She glanced at her watch. "Shoot! We got so busy with customers that I didn't get to the post office in time to get the fabric."

"Hurry up and knock on the door," Sarah said. "You know that Kitty is usually there an hour after closing time, anyway."

"Good point," Melanie said, but her face was lined with stress.

"So I'll let Jason know you're coming to the event?" Sarah confirmed before Melanie could get away. "You know, for someone who has wallowed for months about being single, you are doing very little to try to change your circumstances," she pointed out.

Melanie gave a reluctant smile. "Fair enough." She huffed out a sigh. "Fine. I'll come."

"Jason will pick us up at seven," Sarah said with a smile as she turned to the left toward her apartment and Melanie stayed planted to the sidewalk, still struggling with this information. "You never know. You might meet someone and then you won't have to bring Jason as your date to the wedding!"

Melanie frowned a little. "I don't see that happening."

Me either, Sarah thought, as she turned to go, fighting off a little smile.

*

Melanie hurried to the post office, and Sarah was right, there behind the counter was Kitty, peering at an envelope that she was holding up to the light. She stiffened when Melanie knocked on the glass pane, and set the envelope down quickly.

"Melanie!" Kitty's cheeks were red when she opened the door. "You just caught me making sure that tonight's post was all sealed up tight."

Is that what she was calling it? Melanie pinched her lips and said nothing more on the topic. She'd remember not to let anything too personal come through the post again, at least, not in a white envelope.

"I had a few orders to pick up," Melanie said with a smile. "Do you mind if I get them? Things got a little busy today."

"No problem, dear." Kitty walked back around the counter and began sorting through packages. "More clothing, was it?" Her eyes roamed to Melanie's abdomen, which was already flatter than usual these days thanks to her new diet.

"Just some fabric for a gown I'm making."

"Making?" Kitty's brows shot up. "I thought you only sold gowns at Bayside Brides!"

Melanie shifted on her feet, wondering if she should

have kept quiet, but it was better than explaining that she was not with child. "It's a gift for Abby. You know she's marrying my brother next Saturday."

"I do know," Kitty said. "Not that I was invited."

Melanie stifled a sigh. Such was the downside of small-town life. Everyone knew everyone and everyone had an opinion. Even with a small event, people were bound to be slighted, even if Kitty's connection to anyone in the wedding party was loose at best. Maybe she and Melanie's mother had once volunteered at a festival together. Maybe.

Kitty's eyes darted briefly to Melanie and back to the pile of packages. "Cutting it a bit close, aren't you?"

Like she needed to be reminded. Baring a smile that was braver than she felt, she held out her arms and accepted the packages as Kitty retrieved them, happy to see the return address for the fabric store on the upper left corner of the largest box. "It will all be fine."

And it would be fine. More than fine. It had to be. Not just for Abby and her perfect wedding day, but for Melanie, and for her future.

Chapter Eight

Why had she agreed to this? Melanie stood at the back of the restaurant on Saturday evening, a drink in hand, avoiding eye contact with the dozens of singles who had turned out for the event, mostly women, and a thin crowd at that. She didn't recognize anyone, at least. That was one perk to driving all the way to Shelter Point. Still, instead of feeling hopeful at the prospect of fresh faces, she felt tired and restless.

"I'm surprised you agreed to this," she remarked to Jason, who stayed at her side, even though Sarah had urged them to spread out as soon as they walked through the door, claiming it was the only way to meet new people. She had a point, and Melanie was trying to keep an open mind. She'd worn her favorite earrings and belly-hugging shape wear under her black wrap dress, hoping to hide the damage from so many nights of take-out pizza.

"It was better than going home and being guilt-tripped by my parents," he said affably.

She eyed him steadily. If that was the only reason, couldn't he have just suggested they meet for a drink instead?

Before she could push the topic, the coordinator of the event, a middle-aged woman with stiletto heels and hair that was colored a severe shade of blond, tapped a fork against her wine glass. "Everyone was given a number when you arrived. That will be your first seating. You'll have five minutes with each person. When I ring this bell—" Sure enough she held up a bell. "Ladies, when I ring the bell, you will shift one seat to the left. Remember to mark your cards! Flirt! Have fun! And find your match!"

Oh, good God, it was starting. Melanie looked up at Jason with naked dread. It wasn't too late to leave, go down the street, and come back in an hour when this whole thing was over, was it?

"What number did you get?" Jason asked.

"Two."

"I got eleven. I guess we'd better get to the table."

Melanie didn't know whether to drain her glass and leave it on the bar or bring it with her. She decided to carry it to the long row of tables that were set up down the center line of the room; women on one side, men on the other. This was what it had come to. Because the women outnumbered the men, several had to stand, wait their turn for the next round.

Melanie secretly wished she'd gotten their number instead. She could hide in the bathroom, or take a good read on the scene before calling it quits. Instead, she scooted into her seat, dismayed when a man who was easily as old as her father took the chair opposite. She gave him a shy smile. "Hi—"

He shook his head. "No talking yet. Not until the bell."

A rule monger then. Or perhaps just a veteran. Either way, she didn't feel hopeful that they would hit off.

She suppressed a sigh and looked down the table to Sarah, who was across from a nerdy-looking guy with a pad of paper in his hand, as if he planned to take down notes. Farther up was Jason, across from a pretty-looking blonde. Something in her stomach shifted. She didn't like this. Not one bit.

She scanned the rest of the table. A few decent-looking guys, sure, but she couldn't muster up any excitement, and the thought of trying to summarize her life in five minutes was just stressful. She was out of the game. She didn't know how to flirt or be witty.

And she could already tell that the man across from her was a better match for Dottie Joyce than he was for her.

The bell rang. She listened to the man (Neil) describe his hobbies: golf, bridge club, reading about American history.

She glanced down the table. Jason was laughing at something the blonde was saying. She caught Sarah's eye, who gave her a subtle plea for help by opening her eyes comically wide and keeping them that way.

Melanie raised her eyebrows in return. This had been Sarah's grand idea, after all.

She revealed what she did as vaguely as possible. Co-owned a bridal salon, designed dresses in her spare time, no pets, one brother, no real hobbies unless you counted eating shredded cheese straight from the bag. No, she didn't throw in that last part, but she was tempted, if only to lighten the mood.

Finally, after what felt like fifty minutes rather than five, the bell rang. Melanie scooted to the left. This next man was considerably more attractive and she could just picture her mother's wild-eyed excitement if she were to hit it off with him, bring him home, or even admit that she had come to this event at all. That she had tried.

She needed to try. Her mother was right about that. After all, Doug had moved on while she was sitting in her sweats watching television.

She smiled at the man, opened her mind, and then closed it immediately when he admitted to his four pet ferrets and his love for hunting. "You ever try squirrel meat?" he asked.

Melanie was officially silenced, even if they had another four minutes on the clock. He wasn't a match, and if the ferrets and the hunting hadn't been enough, when he announced that he was a professional "gamer" and lived in his parents' basement, and wondered if she, too, liked video games, she knew that even her mother wouldn't push her on this one.

The nerdy guy that Sarah had been matched up with was next. She was more interested in the notebook that in getting to know him, and spent a fair bit of their time trying to decipher the tiny writing that filled his page. Catching her, he shielded his work, like they used to do back in grade school.

"But you're taking notes about me," she said defensively. "Don't I deserve to know what you wrote?"

He considered this for a moment and finally pushed the book toward her. It said three words only. Not a match.

She blinked at the man, who said nothing as he pulled the notebook back to his side of the table and covered it protectively. "How could you tell that in such a short time?"

"That's why it's called speed dating. This isn't about conversation. This is about instant attraction."

Was it? She supposed he was right. She had a few more guys to get through before the evening was over and she was dreading the thought of five minutes of small talk.

The only guy in the room she really had an interest in talking to was Jason, and she didn't know what to make of that.

*

Jason didn't know why he had agreed to come to this. Scratch that. Yes, he knew *exactly* why he had agreed. Sarah had said that Melanie was coming, and the thought of her spending a Saturday night chatting with other guys meant the thought of sitting around his parents' house and wondering what she was doing would be unbearable. Even more unbearable than listening to his mother drop hints about him coming back to Oyster Bay and joining his dad at the clinic.

He knew he should feel bad for Melanie that the line-up of guys was a list of duds. And he knew he should feel bad that pretty much every woman in the room was going to list him as a match. He couldn't list any of them. Sure, Tiffany had been pretty, and Jen had been funny, and he could maybe see himself getting to know a few of the others better, too, but his heart wasn't in it. It never was, and that was just the problem. He'd go on dates over the years, try to keep an open mind and forge a connection, but all he could think about was the one person who understood him and knew him best, and didn't see him in a romantic light.

How was that for bitter irony?

Instead, it was easier to be single, to immerse himself in his work. When he came back to town, all the feelings stirred up again. Once he was back in Boston he'd settle into his routine. It wouldn't bug him so much anymore.

But it would still be on his mind.

Finally, Melanie slid into the chair opposite him and gave him a wide-eyed look that made him burst out laughing. "I take it that this hasn't been your idea of a perfect Saturday night?"

Her eyes drooped as she looped her handbag onto the back of her chair. "I think my perfect Saturday night would have been a quiet night with a bottle of wine and a hot plate of fettuccine Alfredo. And something chocolate for dessert."

"Sounds ideal," he said. Far more relaxing than the grind of making small talk with over a dozen women, too.

"That's our plan for next time then, if Sarah ever tries to rope us into this again."

"I'd like that," he said, and then, catching her eye, he cleared his throat.

"Do you think Sarah had any luck?" she asked, glancing down the table at her friend, who seemed a little more subdued than she'd been on the car ride over, when she was frantically combing her hair and touching up her lipstick.

"Not sure. How were the guys?" He didn't want to know almost as much as he wanted to brace himself. Melanie was often single, but she also had boyfriends at times. Relationships that never went anywhere and never had a chance of going anywhere and that had been obvious and comforting. Sure, he didn't like the idea of her dating Doug, and he definitely didn't love the way the guy hurt her, but he also knew that Doug wasn't a threat. That he didn't have to worry. That for now, at least,

Melanie was still his.

That wouldn't be the case forever, though. And it definitely wouldn't be if he stayed in Boston indefinitely.

But to come back to Oyster Bay, without reason...

He smiled at her, a secret smile they had shared so many times over the years, as early back as when Mrs. Glen, their seventh-grade teacher, had a peculiar habit of putting on strange voices when she read aloud to the class. It was the same smile he'd given her when she hopped into the car tonight, knowing at once that they were both dreading this, and going along for each other. But still a part of him worried that Melanie wasn't just doing it for him or for Sarah, but for herself.

She wanted to meet someone. She wanted to settle down. And eventually that would happen. And then...He couldn't even think about it.

"What do you say we get a drink when we get back to town?" Melanie said, when the bell finally rang and Sarah came running over to them, looking just as eager to leave as Jason felt.

He knew the event wasn't over yet. They'd have to hand in their cards, see if a match would be made, but his card was blank. He glanced at Melanie's card, but she caught him looking and held it up to her chest.

"What?" He was amused, but a flicker of panic also made him frown. "You can't show me?"

"I'll show you mine if you show me yours," she challenged.

He shrugged. He had nothing to hide, after all. He handed over his card and took hers. It was blank, as he had hoped, and he hated the relief that made the tension roll out of his shoulders.

Her brow knitted when she looked at his. "No one?"

"I'm going back to Boston in a week," he reminded her, and she gave a sad smile as she handed the card back.

"Well, I have a blank card, too," Sarah huffed. Her eyes were darting over the room, in case she missed someone. "I wish we'd never come. It got my hopes up and now they've come crashing down again."

"Come on," Melanie said, as they walked out the door. "Drinks on me tonight. We can go to Dunley's again. Or The Lantern?"

Jason wondered if she was calculating where Doug might be. Was she looking to run into him or avoid him?

Sarah shook her head. "You two go ahead without me tonight. I'm too depressed at the thought of officially having no date for Abby's wedding next weekend. You guys are so lucky to have each other."

Jason and Melanie exchanged a smile. He knew it. But did Melanie?

*

"Think Sarah will be okay?" Jason asked as he held open the door to The Lantern and let Melanie pass first.

She scanned the room, looking for Doug, but it was all clear. The only people at the bar that she recognized were Chip, the owner, and Ron, a regular. It would seem that

Doug had decided to change up his routine and switch to Dunley's, just as he had switched girlfriends.

"It's not easy being single in this town and working in a bridal salon day after day," Melanie said as she slid onto a stool. "I think she's worried about her grandmother, too, even if she's not showing it."

Jason frowned as he scanned the drinks menu. "I'll talk with her some more, then. Alzheimer's can be a scary diagnosis."

Melanie grinned at him until he was forced to look at her. "What?" he asked.

"Look at you," she said, swatting his arm. "It's sweet that you would talk to Sarah about this."

"Well, it's also my job," he said. "For the moment."

"But back in Boston you don't engage with your patients like this," she pointed out. It always baffled her that he could be content with that, but it seemed to fit him, more and more, until she'd forgotten he could be any other way.

"I don't have the opportunity to. The emergency room doesn't allow time to get personal." He sighed. "I haven't told my mom yet that I'm planning to take a full-time job there when my residency is finished."

"Maybe wait and cross that bridge when it's official," Melanie suggested. She smiled at Chip Donovan, who approached with a grin.

"Whatever's on tap for me," Jason said.

"And a glass of white wine for me," Melanie added.

"On the house," Chip said, and brushed away their protests with a wave of his hand. "You all ready for the wedding next weekend?"

Melanie felt a ripple of nerves when she thought of everything she had to do before the big day. Really, she should be home tonight, working on Abby's dress, instead of having a drink with Jason. But Jason was only in town for another week, and the truth was that she was scared to really dive into that dress, to take the shears to that beautiful satin. Even though she'd bought extra, just in case of error, there was something terrifying about committing to the project completely. Sketching was one thing. But actually constructing the dress was another.

"It's certainly an exciting day for my family," Melanie said. "My mother won't admit how nervous she is, but it's a big deal to her."

"Abby isn't even my daughter, but she may as well be. Every time I walk one of my nieces down the aisle it feels as if I'm giving my own away." Chip gave a wistful smile as he handed her the glass of wine. "Just wait until it's your turn. Then your mother will really be feeling the nerves."

"Oh." Melanie gave a small laugh. "I'm not so sure that day will ever come."

"Seems to me you've got a great guy right here next to you," Chip said, giving her a wink. He slid Jason's beer across the table. "I assume you're coming to the wedding?"

"Wouldn't miss it," Jason replied, and Melanie

refrained from pointing out that he almost had. It had hurt her, even though she'd understood. Jason didn't live in Oyster Bay anymore. She could hardly expect him to come back just for her sake.

Even if she wished she could.

"We're going together. As friends," Melanie clarified to Chip.

He gave them a strange little smile before looking over at Ron, who was drowning his feelings again tonight, it would seem; the knitting that he did to keep his anxiety at bay and his fingers distracted from speed dialing his ex-wife was spread out on the wooden surface. Today's project was blue. Pastel. And long. It was either an oversized scarf or a very skinny blanket. Something told Melanie that it wasn't about the end product, but the process.

"What is that about?" Jason asked. His expression was one of such alarm that Melanie couldn't help but laugh.

"The knitting or the comments from Chip?"

He shrugged. "Both, I guess. But then my mom gets the same way about the two of us."

Melanie slid him a suspicious look. "Really?" This was the first he'd ever mentioned such a thing. "My mom, too, actually."

He stared at the bottles that were lined up behind the bar and took a sip of his beer. "Interesting."

"My mom seems to have this theory that we're older now and things have changed. Of course she is reading way too far into us going to this wedding together." She sighed. There would be more explaining this week, of course. More disappointment, no doubt, too.

"My mother thinks if you and I get together, I'll stay in Oyster Bay. Like, maybe you could be my reason." He glanced at her, and back to the bar.

"That's ridiculous," Melanie said after a beat.

"It is. Truly. Ridiculous." Jason agreed, but his voice was throaty and his tone was forced, and Melanie eyed him carefully for a moment before catching his eye and looking away.

"After all, your job is in Boston. You love it there," she pointed out.

"That's right." He looked straight ahead. "I love it."

"So, they're just being ridiculous," she said again, and he nodded, just once, but said nothing more to convince her otherwise.

Yep, ridiculous, she thought, as she sipped her drink. Completely.

Chapter Nine

Jason was relieved that his mother had gone into town when he came downstairs on Sunday morning. His father was on his favorite chair, his remote in his hand, and his meds on the end table beside him, along with a glass of water. Jason knew that his father loved coffee as much as anyone, and it was probably killing him to ease back on it for a while.

He decided to forgo his own cup until he'd had a chat with his father, opting for an orange juice instead.

"Hey, Dad." He gave a small grin as he walked into the room and sat on the leather couch. The news was on, but his father turned it off and rested his hands on his gut. He'd always been a bit out of shape, never had time for the gym, always too busy at the clinic or responding to calls at all hours. He loved what he did, but it had taken its toll. Perhaps it was inevitable, Jason supposed. During his shifts at the hospital, he barely had time to eat, and he'd learned to run on very little sleep. He looked haggard, and older than his years. And he was just starting out. "How are you feeling?"

"Lucky," his father said with a shake of the head. "When stuff like this happens, it's a wake-up call."

"Of course." Sometimes Jason felt like every day of his life was a wake-up call. The cases that came through the emergency room ranged from superficial to dire and he had to work hard not to let any of them hit too close to home. There wasn't always time to react, and certainly no time for emotion to creep in. His job required quick action; half the time the patient was only in his care for a few minutes before going into surgery. And more than half the time after that, he never knew what happened to them. Did they make it? Sometimes he knew they would, but other times he was almost afraid to ask.

"Life is short," his father was saying. "I've been thinking that it's time I really think about how I want to spend it."

Jason nodded, but he wasn't sure what his father meant by this. Dr. Paul Sawyer was a doctor, morning, noon, and night. He didn't spend his time any other way. Unless you counted a round of golf a few times a year.

"And what have you decided?" Maybe this was what his father needed, after all. Maybe now he would finally bring in an extra set of hands, take a step back, or at least cut down on the hours he was putting in.

"I think it might be time to retire, son," his father said simply. He must have seen the shock in Jason's expression, because his eyes drooped into a kind smile.

"Has Mom been pushing for this?" Jason asked, thinking of his mother's ominous statement the other night when Melanie had come to dinner.

"Not pushing, no. But we've certainly discussed it. I haven't made a lot of time for her over the years. My patients have always been my priority. But now I realize that it's important to make myself a priority, too. At least my health. I owe your mother that. I owe you that too."

"But medicine is your life," Jason insisted.

"Medicine is my *career*. And my passion. But not my life." His father gave him a knowing look. "Don't get me wrong, I'll miss it. I've had a good run. But I'm not young anymore, and there are other things I'd like to do before it's too late."

Jason blinked. Of course there had been sacrifices over the years. To hear his father talk like this made him feel like his parents wouldn't be with him much longer. That their golden years were already behind them, or soon would be. He set the orange juice down. His taste for it was lost.

"Your mother always wanted to go on one of those river cruises in Europe. I never had time for it before. Now I think, it's now or never!"

Now or never. Was this some response to post-traumatic stress, or was his father actually serious about his plans?

"And the clinic?" Jason almost didn't want to know. That clinic was like his second home. He'd fed the fish in the tank as a kid, straightened the magazines his mother ordered, and taken the job of carrying charts to and from rooms very seriously on the after school visits his father allowed. It was a part of his life. It was familiar. It was something he'd relied on to always be there. Just like this house. Just like his parents.

"It will be hard to leave it, but, it's time," Paul said, his tone somber but resigned. He flicked back on the television. A news anchor began talking about the stock market.

Jason shook his head. He had no words left. His father had made his decision. His heart was pounding when he thought of all the changes ahead, and after a few minutes of watching the news together in silence, he stood up and went upstairs to his room to grab a light jacket.

He'd get a coffee in town, he decided. And he'd walk there. He needed to clear his head. But something told him that even the fresh air wouldn't be able to cure him today.

*

Sarah called Melanie first thing that morning. "You will never guess who got engaged last night," was all she said.

Oh boy. Melanie went through the list of suspects. "Kelly," she said, thinking of her recent conversation with Beth. Maybe Beth knew something they hadn't.

"Hannah," Sarah said.

Aw, Melanie was happy to hear it. Hannah and Dan had been high school sweethearts. They belonged together. Always had. It was about time, too, since they'd reunited last summer. It was truly meant to be. "I'm happy for them," she said, smiling.

"I am too," Sarah said. "But is it terrible to still feel a little sorry for myself?"

Melanie laughed. "Look at it as another customer. Chloe will be happy." Unless Hannah asked Melanie to make her dress, that was.

Sarah let out a long sigh. "Well, do you mind if I take your shift for the day? I could use a distraction from all this self-pity. Last night was just *so* disappointing."

"You'd be doing me a favor," Melanie said, hanging up the phone. *Thank goodness for that*, Melanie thought with relief. Not only could she dodge Chloe for a day, but she could use the entire day to work on Abby's dress, and she had a meeting with her at five for a first fitting, not of the dress itself, but of the muslin mock-up she'd made of the pattern. It was safer that way; then she didn't have to worry about completing a garment with the expensive fabric without the assurance that Abby was wholly satisfied with how the end product would be.

Plus, she was rusty. She sewed at the shop, but only alterations and minor things like sashes and the occasional torn hem. Creating an entire garment was something she hadn't done in years, since before the shop had opened. Before Chloe had suggested they go into business together, she'd had other dreams and aspirations, plans that now seemed as equally far away as they did far-fetched.

She set the muslin mock-up on the dress figure that had been used as a glorified clothes hanger for the last several years and took a step back to admire it. It felt good to be creating again. And she had Jason to thank for that.

She hadn't had time to go to the grocery store in a couple days and she'd run out of coffee yesterday. Deciding that she deserved a treat for her efforts, though a small one, with the wedding less than a week away, she slipped on her ballet flats and walked the few blocks into the center of town, dreaming of the pastries at Angie's but vowing to only have a biscotti and a coffee instead. She'd worked too hard to turn back now.

She was just stirring the creamer into her cup when she spotted Jason across the room, sitting at a rear table, his back to her.

He was alone, and, when he looked out the window and she caught his profile, he looked troubled. For a moment she wondered if she should leave him be, let him call her, or text, but then she thought, this was *Jason* she was talking about. Her best friend. Her closest person in the entire world.

"Hey." She gave him a little pat on the back as she approached his table. He was solid. He worked out, she knew. There was a gym at the hospital for staff that he hit to blow off steam, but he claimed he rarely had time to use it. Every time Jason described his job, Melanie pictured one of the evening medical dramas she'd become addicted to, especially during her year of being a recluse. She imagined hospital romances, flirtations at the cafeteria, and intimate moments in the break rooms.

She didn't like it. She didn't know why, but she didn't. It was silly, perhaps, to be jealous of Jason giving another woman his company. But none of them could ever know him like she would. Even when he someday married and had kids, wouldn't she be the woman who still knew him best?

But then, she supposed the same could be said for her, if she ever found the one. It was a strange thought, and not one that she was entirely comfortable with. Jason was her person. And she was, well, she was his.

"Hey!" He looked up in surprise at her, and his expression seemed to brighten. Still, she knew him well. There was a shadow in his eyes. Yep, something was definitely troubling him.

"Hiding from your mom again?" She tried the most obvious issue at hand as she pulled out the chair opposite him.

"My dad has decided to retire," he said in a low voice, his eyes skirting to the right to make sure they hadn't been overheard. Of course, news like this would spread like fire, and it wouldn't be well received either.

"*Retire?*" Melanie also dropped her voice to a whisper, but she couldn't hide her shock. Dr. Sawyer was an institution, from his jolly laugh to the stash of lollipops that never seemed to run out, to his calming demeanor, the entire town felt safe with him as their doctor. "Is his health that bad?"

Jason shook his head. He looked tired, she noticed, or perhaps just stressed. "He said the heart attack was a wake-up call. He wants to spend his remaining years doing other things. He wants to take a river cruise. In Europe."

Well, who didn't? Melanie had seen commercials for those cruises every night of her life for the past year, and she always imagined how lovely it would be to enjoy a croissant from the deck, as she floated by Switzerland at a snail's pace.

But right. Back to the issue at hand. Dr. Sawyer could not just retire. What would the people of Oyster Bay do?

"He can't just scale back?" Melanie wondered aloud. She knew, as they all did, that Jason's mother would have loved for him to have joined his father at the practice, while his father had been supportive of Jason getting more experience in Boston.

Still, it was pretty obvious that he was hoping Jason would settle down in Oyster Bay and follow in his footsteps. That's what Jason had always done, after all. It was why he had become a doctor in the first place.

"He says he doesn't want to." Jason tossed up his hands. "Maybe he doesn't think he can. You know how he always puts in extra hours. He's so committed."

"The apple didn't fall far from the tree," Melanie commented, giving him a small smile. "You're hard workers. I can't imagine your father being willing to just leave his patients for extended periods of time."

"No. He's too invested. Always staying late for patients who can't make it during regular office hours."

"And making house calls." Melanie took a sip of her coffee, but it did little to lift her spirits. She sighed, feeling sad and disappointed. So often it felt like nothing changed in Oyster Bay, but then, when something did, it felt like a loss. "They just don't make them like your dad anymore."

Jason's brow knitted as he stared into his mug. "No. I guess they don't." He took a sip. Set the mug down. There was hurt in his eyes, but something else too.

"What has you more upset? That your father has chosen to retire or that the clinic might close down? Everyone retires eventually." She just hadn't pictured Dr. Sawyer ever retiring, though. She doubted that anyone did. He was always so happy, with his big portly belly. He was larger than life. A teddy bear. For a moment she feared she might cry.

"I know, but it's weird to think that he would be willing to put all that behind him. It's hard to think that my parents are slowing down. That an entire phase of their life is behind them, over."

"I doubt he looks at it that way," Melanie said, but knowing how dedicated Jason's father was to his patients and the members of this town, she wasn't entirely sure of this assessment. From the look on Jason's face, he wasn't either.

"Maybe someone else will take over the practice," she said brightly, hoping to lift his spirits. "Then at least the clinic won't have to close down completely."

"We both know that wouldn't be the same," he said, and she nodded sadly. Of course it wouldn't be the same. There would be no lollipops or fish tank and the wallpaper would probably change from the sunny yellow stripes to something grey and depressing and sterile.

"Do you remember the time that Zach and I got in a big fight and he ripped the leg off my stuffed bear and you and I rode our bikes into town and brought it to your father?" She started laughing at the memory. They'd been about nine, and Jason's mother, who had been the receptionist then, had taken down their names and had them wait in a chair, before calling them back to an exam room where Dr. Sawyer expertly sutured the stuffed animal back to health. He gave them both lollipops on the way out. "You promised your father would be able to help and he had. It was also one of the first days I remember you saying that you wanted to be a doctor. To help people."

"With your sewing skills you could have mended that bear eventually," Jason said wryly.

"You're missing the point," she said, exasperated. She took another sip of her coffee. It was growing cold.

Jason raked a hand through his hair. "No, I see the point. It's not a secret that I became a doctor because of my father. It's just hard to see him give it all up. That was his dream."

"Sometimes dreams can change," Melanie pointed out. After all, Jason's had. She thought of her own situation, and smiled. "And sometimes they can be found again. In other ways. At other times."

Jason's gaze was intense across the table. He'd aged in the years he'd been gone. Long hours had taken their toll. There were more lines around his eyes and mouth, but he was still handsome, still achingly familiar. Still rock solid.

Would it be selfish for her to suggest that he consider taking over his father's practice? He loved his job in Boston. He'd made it his priority for a reason. It had changed him, not for the better, but not for the worse either.

They'd grown up, she thought sadly. They'd followed their dreams, and shifted them a little, and maybe they'd even gotten a little off path.

She knew she had. And speaking of…

"I should head out soon. Abby's coming by later for a fitting."

"So you are still moving forward with it then." Jason managed a smile, and he looked so genuinely pleased for her that Melanie felt her heartstrings pull. "I wasn't sure if you'd let Chloe talk you out of it."

"You know Chloe," Melanie said with a sigh, and she didn't need to explain further. Of course Jason knew, and not just because he had grown up with Chloe too, but because he'd been there all the times that she and Melanie had butted heads.

"Maybe you just need to frame your approach in a way that appeals to Chloe," Jason suggested. "Something that will lessen her anxiety."

Melanie thought about this for a minute. He had a point. And as usual, it was a good one. "She has her reasons for being nervous about expanding the business, and believe me, I see the risks, but…"

He raised his eyebrows. "But?"

"This is what I always wanted to do," she said, a little hesitation in her voice.

"It is. And you lost sight of that." He looked at her sternly.

"I got caught up in the daily grind. We're so busy most days we can barely keep up."

"But now you have Sarah," he pointed out. "And I think there was more to it than the daily grind. "

Melanie set her mug down on the table. "What do you mean by that?"

"I mean that it wasn't the shop that made you stop sketching and designing. It was that guy you were dating right after college. He was going to take you to New York and you were going to pursue your dreams and then he broke up with you and then you stopped designing. And then Chloe asked you to partner with her at the shop and the rest, as they say, is history."

Melanie stared at him. He was right. About all of it. "I'd forgotten that," she said, even though of course she hadn't forgotten it at all. Scott was just one of a handful of guys who had broken her heart over the years, and the promises he'd made her weren't forgotten either. "I really stopped designing then?"

But she didn't need him to confirm what she already knew. "Well, thanks for the reminder," she said, giving a tight laugh. "I guess it's easy to lose sight of what we always wanted as we move through life."

He nodded, his expression pensive. "It is," he said.

She tipped her head. "But aren't you doing what you love? You love the action of the emergency room."

"True," he said, but there was doubt in his voice that hadn't been there a few days ago.

"You having second thoughts?" she asked him, wondering if the hope had crept into her voice.

"No, definitely not," he said, straightening in his chair.

"You have everything you ever wanted," she reminded him, even if his original vision had been a little different of course.

"Right," he said, giving her a strange look. "Everything I ever wanted."

*

Abby came over twenty-five minutes early. "I hope that's okay. I can wait outside if you're not ready. I was just so excited and—"

"It's fine," Melanie assured her, opening her door wider to let her future sister-in-law enter her cramped living space. When Zach had moved back to town, he'd stayed with her for a bit, but it was cramped and crowded and that had been a rather bleak period, post break-up and all that. Now she kept the curtains open and the sunshine pouring in and the fridge was stocked with fresh fruits and veggies, after she popped into the Corner Market on her way home from Angie's.

"How was the brunch today?" She'd been using her table for a work space, but it was all cleaned up now, and she'd even put some fresh daffodils in a mason jar in the center. Why wait for a guy to buy you flowers when you could buy some for yourself?

"Busy. I made a stuffed French toast and rosemary hash browns and—"

"Stop!" Melanie could feel her mouth watering. "I'm on a diet. You're making me hungry."

"A diet? Is this because of Doug?"

Melanie bit her lip. Guilty as charged. "Yes. No. I guess it was a wake-up call," she said, thinking of what Jason had said of his father. "I don't want to spend another year sitting on my butt eating chips and feeling sorry for myself."

"You've gotten it out of your system," Abby said with a nod. She grinned. "You look fantastic, by the way."

It had only been a week and Melanie knew that she probably hadn't lost any noticeable weight, but she was happier, lighter, and that must have been what Abby was picking up on. She'd take it.

"Ready to see the mock-up?" Without further delay, she swung open her bedroom door to reveal the most stunning dress constructed of muslin that she'd personally seen. She watched as Abby gasped and clasped a hand to her mouth, her big green eyes shining bright.

"Can I try it on?"

"Of course you can try it on. You have to try it on." Melanie laughed.

Being the youngest of three sisters, Abby wasted no time shedding her clothes and slipping on the garment— something Melanie would have never done but found amusing.

"It's perfect," Abby said, as she admired herself in the full-length mirror that hung from the back of Melanie's closet door.

Melanie grabbed a stash of pins. "Hold still. I see a few areas that need adjusting."

Abby did as she was told, smiling at her reflection. "So will you start making other dresses, then? For the shop?"

Melanie pinched the back of Abby's waist and carefully pushed the pin through the fabric. "I'm still working that out. Chloe can be stubborn, but I suppose I can be too."

"But you're so good at it!"

"Well, it's not always about what you're good at."

"It's important to follow your heart," Abby corrected her.

"Are we talking about our careers or men?" Melanie asked with a laugh. She set her hands on Abby's shoulders and rotated her slightly, before crouching down to inspect the front hem length.

"Both? You won't be happy if you just do what's practical all the time. Sometimes you have to take a leap of faith."

That was easy for Abby to say now that everything had fallen in place for her. Still, she had a point.

"I guess when you try and fail enough times you start to give up hope. Or stop trying."

"Now it's my turn to ask if we're talking about careers or guys," Abby said with a laugh.

"Both," Melanie said, as she set the last few pins into the dress. She'd made a clean pattern, and she felt excited at the idea of starting on the real dress once Abby left. "But right now focusing on my career is a good distraction. And…it's good for me. I probably never would have gotten back into this if you hadn't asked me to make the dress."

"Well, I can't thank you enough," Abby said as she gingerly removed the garment full of pins.

"Thank Jason," Melanie said. She took the dress from Abby, holding it carefully. "He talked me into doing it for you."

A strange look played over Abby's expression as she slipped back into her shoes. "Jason's always been good for you."

"He's my plus one for the wedding, by the way."

"Your mom told me," Abby said, barely suppressing a smile as she picked up her handbag.

"What's that look for?" Melanie asked, following her friend back into the living room.

"Nothing," Abby said. "But it's funny how things all find a way of working out in the end, isn't it? Doug got invited to the wedding, and so you had to ask Jason. And my dress got ruined, and now you're making me a dress, and maybe you never would have if Jason hadn't talked you into it. Seems to me that it was the perfect time for Jason to come back to Oyster Bay."

"He's here because his father had a heart attack!" Melanie reminded her.

"Life has a funny way of sometimes making everything work out as it should, that's all I'm saying." Abby gave her a quick hug and then disappeared out the front door, fluttering her fingers, her grin positively mischievous.

Honestly! Melanie closed the door with a huff. Abby was just getting carried away. She was speaking as a blissful bride to be.

Melanie shouldn't listen to a word she was saying, really.

She really shouldn't. But somehow, when she looked at the beautiful fabric on her coffee table waiting to be cut and thought of how much had changed in just one week, she couldn't stop thinking of everything Abby had said.

And she couldn't stop thinking of Jason.

Chapter Ten

The clinic wasn't technically open until eight, but when Jason arrived at the Victorian home at the edge of Main Street that had housed his father's practice since before Jason was even born, there was an elderly man waiting on the porch.

"Hello," Jason said, giving him a hesitant smile. "Can I help you?" From a quick assessment he didn't appear to be injured or in distress, but there was something in his face, confusion, or anguish, that made Jason stop and turn.

It was Wally Jennings, he realized. He hadn't seen Wally in years, but he'd heard from his parents that the man had been diagnosed with dementia some time ago.

"I'm here to see Dr. Sawyer," Wally replied in a gruff voice. He gave Jason the once-over, clearly not remembering who he was. In fairness, it had been a long time since the two had crossed paths, and last they had, Jason was younger, fitter, and a little less scruffy.

"I'm Dr. Sawyer," Jason said, before he realized that of course the man meant his father. "My father is on medical leave. I'm filling in. Is there something I can do for you?"

"Dr. Sawyer always has me come early," Wally said, looking anxious. He raked his eyes over Jason. "You sure you're a doctor? What are you? Twelve?"

Jason managed a wry smile. It wasn't the first time he had heard a comment like this. "Not for a long time, and yes, I am a real doctor. Why don't we step inside?"

Wally nodded and followed him inside. Jason flicked on the lights in the reception area, knowing that Shelby would arrive soon enough to water the plants and brew the coffee and get him up to speed on his appointments for the day.

Wally hesitated in the lobby. "Your father isn't coming in today then?"

Jason shook his head as he pulled the blinds and let the sunlight fill the room. He'd spoken briefly with his father on the topic of his retirement last night, while watching the ball game. His father would return, but only for a month, and then…Well, and then he was going to Europe!

Jason had nodded silently. A month. Really, what could he say to that? The man's mind was made up, and who was he to contradict or try to convince him otherwise? Besides, if he pressed then his father might start dropping the same hints his mother was. He hadn't yet, but that didn't mean it wasn't on his mind.

Or Jason's.

He pulled in a breath. Nonsense. This clinic had served its time. Jason had moved on. He couldn't expect everything here to stay the same forever, a relic of when he'd left it.

"He'll be back next Monday," Jason offered to Wally, who seemed hesitant to come into an exam room. Frowning, Jason walked over to the appointment book. Shelby always kept a double entry of every appointment: the electronic and physical calendars were always in sync. He scanned the book now, seeing no formal mention of Wally.

It wasn't uncommon, per se. His father had a big heart like that. If Wally was the type who preferred to stop by for a visit, his father would meet with him. Chances were he didn't even charge him.

"I'll come back then, if you don't mind. Your father and I like to start the week with a game of chess. I don't want to break my record."

Jason grinned. That sounded like something that his father would do. Not just because it helped him to keep an eye on Wally without working the man up, but because he and Wally probably had a genuine friendship. His father was unconventional that way. His patients weren't just numbers. They were people.

Jason felt his jaw set. It had been a long time since he

could say the same.

"I'll tell him you dropped by," Jason said, as the man let himself out. He walked to the fish tank, remembering how his favorite thing to do when he came to the office was to sprinkle the food on the surface of the water and watch as all the fish swam to find it, their mouths open.

Now he wondered what would happen to the fish when his father retired. What would happen to everything here?

"Well, good morning!" The only nurse at the clinic, Doreen, was always cheerful when she came through the door, just as she had been twenty years ago, except now her hair was grayer. Did she know about the retirement or suspect it? Would she want to retire herself? She was a part of this place, nearly as much as his father had been.

"Hello, hello." Ah, and there was Shelby, only five years into the job and still perky. At first, Jason wasn't sure that his father would like having a different woman as his assistant, instead of Jason's mother, but Shelby was youthful and energetic and she had a way of making the little kids feel better, even before they went into an exam room. Sadly, it would seem that Jason's mother's plan to spark an early retirement had backfired.

Jason forced a smile and stepped away from the tank. "Good morning. Just checking on the fish."

"Thanks for the reminder. I have to stop at the store on my lunch break and pick up some more food for them." Shelby hooked her bag on the coat rack behind her desk. "I see we're low on lollipops. Should I get some of those too?"

Jason frowned. "I guess. Does my father still do that?"

"The patients look so forward to them," Doreen chimed in enthusiastically. "Even the adults. I've seen grown men needing vaccinations comforted by the thought of a piece of candy at the end of the visit." She laughed, and Jason did too.

"Go ahead and get them," he said to Shelby. He was about to say that just because he was filling in, nothing had changed, but that wasn't exactly true anymore, was it? A lot would soon change, whether a new doctor came in or a new doctor didn't. Either way, this office, the staff, and the comfort the patients took in the practice would be gone. Different. Or just…nonexistent.

He watched Doreen take a stack of charts and walk toward an exam room.

"Shelby," he asked, leaning into the desk while the receptionist settled herself into her chair. "Where do the patients go on weekends if they need a doctor?"

She gave him a funny look. "You know your father. If someone calls, he will come in for them. Or pay them a visit. He's dedicated."

That he was. "But if it's late at night? There must be another place."

She made a little face. "There's the clinic at St. Francis. I brought my daughter there one time for an ear infection when I didn't want to bug your father—it was your parents' wedding anniversary and he had absolutely promised your mother, and Doreen and me, that he would turn off his phone for the night. Anyway. Horrible, sterile place, if you ask me. Grey walls. No music. The doctors barely look you in the eye much less bother to learn your name. You may as well just take a number."

His mouth thinned. Sounded like the place where he worked, basically. He'd liked the clinical aspect of it, the challenge, the belief that he was helping people, but now…Now he wondered just how much help he was offering. How much more could be giving.

Like Wally Jennings, he thought.

Jason walked into his father's office and for the first time closed the door. But instead of getting the privacy he was looking for, he found himself staring at dozens of cards, drawings, thank you letters that had been taped to the back of it. They were all addressed to his father, and they were all letters of thanks.

He crept forward, looking at the crude crayon drawing of a little boy with a broken arm, with a big smile on his face and a lollipop in his hand. At the picture of a woman and a newborn baby, giving her thanks for a successful early delivery. At the picture of a toy bear with his leg sewed back on, and two smiling children clasping hands.

Melanie and him.

Shelby was right. The people of this town did love Dr. Sawyer and they would react badly when he retired. He wasn't just their doctor. He was a legacy.

It wasn't about the lives he had saved. It was about the ones he touched.

*

Because Melanie couldn't bear the thought of another Monday meeting with tension, she decided to smooth things over with Chloe with an offering of pastries from Angie's. The bakery box sat in the center of the storage room table, the treats mostly untouched, and Melanie had to keep looking away from them because that chocolate croissant was just calling to her, screaming really, and with the wedding now just days away, she was determined to stay strong if it killed her. And right now, with the way her stomach was grumbling, it felt like it just might. She solaced herself with the thought of a raspberry yogurt after the meeting, before the shop opened for business.

They went over the usual business first: status updates of all clients, orders that needed to be placed or were outstanding (never good), and thoughts on the fall catalogues, which they had all had a chance to browse by now.

"I loved this ball gown with the three-quarter-length sleeves," Chloe said, flipping to a page she had bookmarked in the catalogue. Chloe never earmarked, and poor Sarah had learned that lesson before Melanie had even had a chance to warn her. Now they could laugh about the gasp of horror that could be heard over the classical music that played at an admittedly low volume in the store during business hours.

Melanie glanced at the dress. It was traditional, in a rich, creamy satin, and a heavily beaded bodice. "Works for me."

Chloe looked at her suspiciously. "Unless you had other ideas?"

Melanie swallowed hard. Typically they tossed out a few ideas for the season's display, often changing it each month. She wondered if Chloe could be testing her right now. Or if she was just being paranoid because she hadn't looked at the catalogues yet.

"I like it," Sarah said uneasily, glancing at each of them. "I also liked this one." She pulled out another catalogue and flipped to a page she, too, had bookmarked. "This one. If I ever get married, this is my dress." She tapped the photo with determination.

Chloe laughed. "You say that about every dress."

Melanie leaned forward and admired the frothy tulle skirt and the cascade of crystals that faded to the bottom. It had long mesh sleeves and a scoop neck overlay bodice with exquisite stone work in a dainty pattern. "That's lovely."

Chloe lifted an eyebrow. There were three months to each season, and it was Melanie's turn to contribute. She held up her hands. She couldn't lie. "I haven't had a chance to narrow down my selections yet."

Chloe didn't look surprised. "Too busy working on a custom dress?" She closed the catalogues and began stacking them, neatly.

"As a matter of fact, yes. The fall orders are important, but we have a month at least." She pulled in a breath. "The wedding is this weekend."

"And your extracurricular project is taking precedence over your job."

"It's a gift to the bride, yes, but it's also a reason to get back to designing. You know that's what I always wanted to do, Chloe. I'm not willing to drop the conversation of expanding the business."

Sarah made a grand gesture of taking a huge bite from the chocolate croissant. She was purposefully keeping her mouth full, no doubt, to avoid being asked for her opinion.

"How is the dress coming?" Chloe surprised her by asking.

Melanie hesitated, unsure where Chloe was going with this. She'd starting pinning the dress last night and she hoped to have the sewing completed tonight, even if she had to drink a pot of coffee to stay up. She didn't want to leave anything until the last minute, and hopefully over the next few days, all she would have to worry about were the embellishments and finishing touches.

"Good." She nodded. "And Abby commissioned Beth to make a necklace and earrings. Of course she bought that through the store, though, so we'll get a portion of the sale, and the dress, well…"

Melanie pulled in a breath and retrieved the estimated income she felt the dress would have brought them, if it hadn't been a gift to the bride. She'd worked carefully on the spreadsheet, calculating the cost of materials and her time, and how much she thought the dress could sell for.

The idea had come to her after her talk with Jason. Chloe was anxious, scared about profits, losing money, losing the business. Melanie had to appeal to her senses. This was the best way. Maybe the only way.

She slid the paper across the table to Chloe, who looked at it in silence for what felt like an excruciatingly long period of time.

Chloe chewed her lip. "Interesting," she said, and Melanie and Sarah exchanged a glance.

Melanie waited for Chloe to hand the paper back to her, but instead, she tucked it inside the portfolio she always kept at her right side in these meetings.

Melanie fought back a smile. She'd call that progress.

*

On a whim, Jason decided to stop by Bayside Brides, not just because he was avoiding going home, but because he realized that in less than a week he would be gone, and he already missed Melanie just thinking about it.

She was crouched on the floor, fluffing a ridiculously huge wedding gown skirt, five pins held in her mouth, which made him cringe. Quickly she pinned the hem and glanced his way, mouthing something he couldn't quite discern but he assumed she was asking him to wait.

He wandered to the counter, where Chloe was frowning at the computer screen. "Hello there," he said, giving her a warm smile.

She cocked an eyebrow at him. "I hear you're behind

all the trouble that's been brewing here in the store."

"Me?" He couldn't have been more surprised at the accusation, but then he remembered that despite Abby asking Melanie to make her dress, he had technically been the one who encouraged her to do it. Sarah had been deliberately neutral, hadn't she?

He glanced around for her, a friendly face as back-up, but she didn't appear to be working at the moment.

"Don't deny it," Chloe said, but a small smile played at her mouth. "But then, I suppose Abby is to blame, too. She has a knack for getting her way. But then, Melanie's always had a soft spot for you."

"I'd like to think that I simply facilitated a conversation," he said, careful not to push too hard. "And I like seeing Melanie happy and living her life to its fullest potential."

"What's this about seeing me happy?" Melanie was at his side, her smile radiant, her eyes lit up in a way that made his stomach flip over. When she looked at him like that…Well, she probably shouldn't. It filled him with hope, and she'd never given any real reason to place it there. "What brings you to the store?"

"I thought I'd stop by, see if you were getting off soon."

Her eyes darted to Chloe. "I had some work to do tonight, but I could spare a little time. Give me five minutes to finish up here?"

"Go ahead," Chloe said. She shook her head, but she

was smiling. "Five minutes won't ruin the business or anything."

"That's very flexible of you, Chloe!" Melanie remarked, but she gave her cousin a wink and a quick hug before grabbing her bag from under the counter and linking Jason's arm.

He felt his body stiffen, his every nerve awakened at the casual gesture. It was nothing new, but it was exciting every time. Even now, after all these years.

"Where are we headed?" she asked when they stepped outside.

He shrugged. "The beach?" A walk on the beach always cleared his head, and right now, he needed some peace, or some distraction, or maybe a little of both.

They talked about the wedding plans as they walked to the end of Main Street and down the wooden steps that led to the sand. Pale pink dresses. A last minute change to the flowers, which Melanie had to admit was for the better. He tried to listen, but his mind was wandering.

The ocean was turbulent today, and the waves crashed at the shoreline. It was a cool day for spring, and the only other soul to be spotted was a man and his dog, a big black lab, far out in the distance.

Melanie kicked off her shoes and set them in her bag. "Summer will be here soon."

Summer. That's when he would likely start his permanent position in Boston. By then, who knew what would become of the clinic. Would it already be sold off? Or torn down?

"I used to look forward to the summers," he said, thinking back on those carefree days. "Remember how we used to ride our bikes until the sun went down?"

"We could make five bucks last all day," she added. "And that included ice cream and some penny candy—"

"And pool fare." He laughed. "Life was so simple then. I miss those days."

"Then come back," she said, simply, naturally.

"You make it sound as if it's just that easy," he said. The sand was cold against his bare feet, but Melanie didn't seem to mind.

"Would it be so bad? To come back? To spend our weekends like we did before?"

"Riding bikes and eating sweets until we felt sick?" He laughed.

She stopped walking and looked at him properly. The sun was low in the sky and her eyes seemed to glow. She was radiant. She was beautiful. She was everything he'd ever wanted and she didn't even know. And maybe that was the problem. Maybe she should have known. Maybe everything would have been different if she had.

Her dark brown hair blew in the breeze, licking across her face, and he reached out, gently pushed the strands back, fighting with them against the wind. She laughed, but stopped when her gaze caught his. He looked at her, opened his mouth, decided that he was going to tell her here and now, or maybe just kiss her, lean in and do the one thing he'd always wanted to do and hadn't yet.

Because of their friendship. Because he couldn't bear the thought of losing her completely, even if, in some ways, he had only ever guaranteed that someday, when some wonderful, worthy man came along, he would.

He leaned in, and she blinked up at him, and just like that, his entire body stiffened. There was so much to lose, too much perhaps, and their time had come and gone, their decisions made. He was going back to Boston in only a few days. And Melanie…Well, Melanie didn't see him that way, never had.

He cleared his throat, stepped back, and fell into step beside her again.

Eventually, it was Melanie who broke the silence. "Thanks for coming with me to the wedding, by the way. I know I've thanked you before, but you're doing me a big favor, truly."

A favor. Of course. He nodded, grinned at her, felt his entire chest roll over. "Happy to be at your side."

She locked his eyes for a moment and looked away. "So any chance of you coming back this summer?"

"To…ride bikes and catch fireflies?"

"Oh!" she exclaimed. "I loved those fireflies!"

And I loved you, he thought. Instead he shrugged, feeling torn and restless and as uneasy as he had before he'd stopped to see her. More so even. "Maybe I will come back," he said. "This summer."

"That would be great!" she exclaimed. "It would be just like old times!"

Old times. Meaning nothing would change. Nothing

would move forward. He wouldn't move forward.

"Maybe for a weekend," he said, forcing a grin. They made their way back up the beach, and Melanie gave a sad sigh, one that he would definitely not be reading into.

She wanted him to stay. But not for the right reasons. Not for the one that would keep him here.

Chapter Eleven

On Wednesday evening, at five sharp, the same time she came every week, Sarah pulled up to Serenity Hills and let out a sigh. This is where it would all end for her, she was starting to realize. No spouse to grow old with. No children to take care of her. No grandchildren to bake cookies with or oversee her final wishes. She would die alone, eaten by cats, if she were so inclined to get them, though she had always preferred dogs. Or she would expire here, in a single bed with a game show playing on the television that would become her sole source of company, or in the cafeteria, because despite how decent their dinners could be, their breakfast eggs were so dry that it was possible she might choke on them and Marie or one of the other nice ladies in hairnets would feel eternally responsible, and she didn't want that. She didn't want any of it.

She was being dire, she knew, but she was also feeling low. She used to think of Serenity Hills as a nice place, a safe establishment and a good fit for her grandmother, but now even the daffodil-lined path to the front door couldn't brighten her spirits.

She supposed she should have known that the speed dating event would be a bust. She had set her expectations too high, even though she'd promised herself that she would do no such thing. She'd worn her best skirt, pink and flirty, with a white top and some costume jewelry that Abby had let her keep when she was packing up her apartment to move in with Zach. Abby was always trying to help her shake up her love life or help her look her best, just in case pigs started flying and a cute eligible bachelor just happened to be walking down Main Street. And it hadn't mattered. Sarah was beginning to think that instead of going to the speed dating event, she would have been better off going over to the pharmacy and chatting with poor Tim. Even with his enlarged Adam's apple, nervous twitch, and overbearing mother, he was more desirable than any of the guys she'd had five minutes of small talk with had been, and that was saying a lot. Well, other than Jason, of course, but he wasn't an option.

It was more than obvious that he only had eyes for Melanie.

She sighed as she pushed open her car door, grabbed

the box of chocolate-chip cookies she'd bought in town, and walked into the building, scanning the lobby for her grandmother. Usually when Esther knew that Sarah was going to stop by, she waited for her at the front bay window, in the big, blue, wingback chair that held her posture nicely. She usually wore lipstick just for the occasion, something that saddened Sarah as deeply as it touched her.

But today her grandmother was not in the lobby, and a man she didn't recognize (a newcomer, quite possibly) was sitting in her chair. Giving a wave to the woman at the visitor's desk, she went straight through to the elevator and took it to the second floor, where her grandmother had lived ever since she had asked to be relocated from the first floor, after her little squabble with Abby's grandmother that, fortunately for Abby and Sarah's friendship, had ended amicably. Now the two women had their nails and hair done each Tuesday at the onsite salon.

That's right, Sarah reminded herself as she walked down the hall to her grandmother's room. There was a salon here. And a garden. And a game room. And people cooked three meals a day for you, and you didn't have to clean up, and that was a pretty sweet arrangement, even if the eggs were dry.

Maybe it wouldn't be so bad after all.

She heard her grandmother's peal of laughter when she was still four doors away. She froze, wondering what had caused it, finally deciding that she was probably laughing at something on the television (her grandmother could get quite grumpy with the staff, unfortunately) and was rather looking forward to seeing what was playing. A rom-com, perhaps? She could use a little pick-me-up, after all, not just from the disappointment of the speed dating event and the looming realization that she was probably (more like most definitely) going to be one of the only single people at Abby's wedding this Saturday, but because things at Bayside Brides were crazy tense lately.

She quickened her step as the laughter continued, but froze when she heard another voice. A deep voice. A man's voice.

Her mind raced. Grandma couldn't have found a male suitor, could she have? It was possible, of course. There had been that man Mitch LaMore who a few of the ladies were after for a while, and then of course Abby's grandmother had met Earl and even married him, right out back in the garden last year!

Feeling uneasy with what she was about to walk into, Sarah gingerly reached for the doorknob and pushed it open a crack, wincing as she poked her head around the door.

"Jason?" She blinked. Sure enough, sitting there, in the visitor's chair, was Dr. Jason Sawyer himself. He looked nearly as surprised as she no doubt did, and, dare she say, a bit embarrassed too.

"That's *Dr. Sawyer*," her grandmother pressed. "Are

those cookies?"

Sarah and Jason exchanged a small smile as she stepped into the room and handed over the bakery box. "Chocolate chip. Plenty for everyone."

Her grandmother snorted. "If you say so. I count only six here and last time you polished off four."

Now it was Sarah's turn to go red in the face. "I was having a bad day," she said hotly.

"And the time before?" Her grandmother looked at her pertly.

Much to her relief, Jason cleared his throat. "Your memory is quite sharp today, Mrs. Preston. I'm pleased to see that."

When the doctors at the hospital had explained her condition, her grandmother hadn't believed them, claimed she was sharp as a knife and that there was nothing wrong with her, and Sarah had been afraid to mention it since. Now she frowned as she studied the exchange between her grandmother and Jason. She'd missed something. More than a little something, she judged. After all, hadn't Melanie insisted that Jason had no bedside manner?

"I'll save these for after dinner, if you don't mind, dear." Her grandmother's tone softened as her smile turned a little sly. "Jason was thoughtful enough to bring me some cherry cordials."

"Your favorite," Sarah remarked. She looked at Jason, impressed. "Lucky guess."

"Oh, I told him, of course." Her grandmother gave a

knowing smile and lowered her voice to a stage whisper. "You always have to drop a few hints to let the men know what you want, my dear. They sometimes need a little push."

Sarah tossed an apologetic glance at Jason, who was doing a very good job of holding back his laughter by studying the television guide with extreme interest.

"I let him know last time he visited," her grandmother continued.

Last time? Sarah knew she couldn't keep the shock from showing in her face. One look at Jason showed a man who wasn't exactly comfortable having this conversation right now. Sarah decided to cut the guy a break. After all, there was no telling what kind of conversation had been going on before she walked in. For all she knew, her grandmother had proposed marriage. She wouldn't put it past her.

"I might run down to the lobby and get a coffee to go with those cordials," she said, glancing at Jason.

He nodded. "I'll join you."

"Hurry back, kids!" her grandmother called as they hurried out of the room.

"Kids?" she looked up at Jason.

"A good sign. We are kids to her." He thrust his hands into his pockets as they walked toward the elevator.

"So...since when do you make house calls?" she asked.

Jason pressed the elevator button and the doors

opened in front of them. "It's what my father does."

"But you're not your father," Sarah pointed out as they stepped inside.

"No, but I feel like I owe it to him to do his job the way he would have done it. And I owe it to his patients, too. I was driving by Monday night so I stopped in to check on her. She seemed to enjoy my visit, and she dropped some pretty big hints about those cordials."

Sarah laughed. She could just picture it. "Well, you have the patience of a saint to visit my grandmother. She isn't always the easiest woman to get along with. I'm not sure if you're aware, but she has earned quite the reputation around here. She and Abby's grandmother engaged in a few food fights, and my grandmother had her reported to security for picking a flower once."

He grinned. "She's a spirited woman and it's my pleasure to check in on her. This won't be an easy process. Do you have any other family around?"

Sarah nodded. "My parents visit, and they're planning a trip here next weekend when they have more time to see me, once the wedding is over."

"That will be nice."

Sarah scrunched up her nose. "Nice probably isn't how I would describe it. I'm an only child and, well, it can be a bit much at times."

The doors opened and he let her pass. "Tell me about it. I'm an only child too. Since I've been back, I feel like my every move has been monitored. It's easier being in Boston."

Sarah felt relief that someone else understood. "It's been easier for me since I moved here. I used my grandmother as an excuse, but the truth was that I needed to try something on my own, and Oyster Bay is a nice town, even if the romantic options are a bit limited."

"No luck finding a date for the wedding?" He seemed to have no trouble finding the café at the back of the facility for a man who had only been here twice. Clearly, he'd familiarized himself with the establishment, or treated himself to a coffee the last time he was here.

"No." Sarah sighed as they joined the line of guests and residents waiting to order. "I considered going with Tim, but—"

"Too nice?" Jason grinned.

"Too something, that's for sure." Sarah laughed. "I'm afraid I don't have a Jason in my life to go with either."

"A Jason?" He cocked an eyebrow at her.

"You know, a perfect man in the form of a best friend to take you to prom and to weddings and to keep you company on holidays and make you laugh and just be by your side?"

"When you put it like that, it's amazing Melanie hasn't married me yet."

Sarah thought about this for a moment, and decided to go for it. "It is strange, isn't it?" She narrowed her gaze on him, letting it linger.

Jason's jaw seemed to set and he didn't look at her. "It's like we said. Melanie likes the bad guys."

"And you?"

He shrugged, but his smile seemed strained. "It doesn't matter what I like, does it?"

She opened her mouth, out of surprise, and then to say something, she wasn't sure what, but something to tell him that it did matter, it should matter, and that maybe he should be sure of that, but a man with a walker shuffled past them and caught his coat on a corner of a table and it didn't take long before he lost his balance and went down, not hard, but enough to warrant Jason's attention.

He was quick to crouch down, instruct the man not to move, and ask if anything hurt.

"Son, I am ninety-six years old. Everything hurts," the man replied sharply.

Jason glanced up at her. "Sarah, I should—"

She dismissed him with a wave. "I'll keep my grandmother company," she said.

"Thank you," he said, and went back to tending to the man, his brow knitting in concern as he checked the man's pupils, asked him his name, and helped him into a chair.

Sarah smiled to herself as she left the café. Melanie didn't think Jason had any bedside manner, and she couldn't have been more wrong. And she also thought that Jason only saw that prom date and this wedding date as a pity date, a favor, and it was pretty clear that she was wrong about that too.

But who would set her right? Sarah thought about this as she walked back to her grandmother's room, shaking her head at how silly her friend could be. She'd been pining for someone who had been right there all along. And he couldn't be more perfect for her.

*

Melanie's eyes burned from lack of sleep. She'd finished the dress in the early hours, and she had barely made time to shower and have a quick coffee before going into the shop and dealing with what felt like extraordinarily shrill brides for a weekday. The finishing touches would all have to be taken care of tonight, preferably by midnight, and then... Her eyes drooped when she thought of her bed.

Her bell rang just as she was starting another pot of coffee, and her pulse sped up for a moment when she considered it was probably Jason. It had been awkward the other night when she'd said goodnight, and Jason had seemed quiet and resigned. And then there had been that weird business of him brushing the hair from her cheek and leaning in, just a fraction, but enough to make her wonder if—

Nonsense! She walked to the door and opened it, hoping the disappointment didn't show on her face when she saw that it was Sarah.

"That happy to see me, huh?" Sarah's blue eyes crinkled, and even though her tone was light, she looked a little hurt.

"Not at all! Happy! I was just about to take a break."

Melanie held the door wider, ushering her inside.

"If you're sure." Sarah looked hesitant as she walked into the living room. "For a moment I was wondering if you were hoping I was someone else."

"Who else?" Melanie quipped, but her tone sounded forced, even to her own ears, and she knew that Sarah was onto her.

"Oh, maybe Jason…" Sarah set her bag on the couch and looked over at Melanie innocently.

Melanie forced a frown. She could feign confusion all she wanted, but Sarah had homed in on the truth. She *had* been hoping to see Jason. She hadn't seen him since Monday night, and even though they'd texted, it wasn't the same. Just like video chats and phone calls weren't the same. She needed him. Face to face. In person. She…needed him.

"I finished the dress!" She needed to change the subject. She needed to think about something other than men. She needed to focus on her career. Her passion. Herself. She'd gotten away from that for too long. Possibly forever. "Well, almost. I just need to serge it and then finish adding some of the beadwork around the neck and waistline."

"Do you think you'll get it done in time?"

"I have no choice!" Melanie stretched her fingers. They had been cramping since yesterday morning. "Luckily Abby wanted something simple, not too ornate, and with any luck, there won't be too many alterations."

"When does she come over for the final fitting?"

Melanie paused and gave her a knowing look. "Tomorrow. At the shop."

They locked eyes for a long moment. "What is Chloe going to have to say about that?"

Melanie shrugged and started making some coffee. "What can she say?" Still, she thought about asking Abby to come after hours. It would make everything…easier.

Sarah's eyes rounded but she said nothing more. She was a smart employee, staying out of the tiff with the bosses, but as a friend, Melanie would have loved her support. Deep down, she knew she had it.

"Coffee?"

Sarah nodded. "I was going to have one at Serenity Hills but didn't get a chance."

"How's your grandmother doing?" Melanie asked as she scooped the grounds into the filter.

"Oh, fine. We chatted a little. I brought some cookies. She accused me of eating too many." Sarah lifted a scrap of fabric and twirled it on her finger. "Jason was there."

Melanie pulled two mugs from the cabinet. "*Jason* was there? And you're just telling me this now?"

Sarah gave a little shrug. "I didn't realize that you cared so much about Jason's comings and goings."

"I do not care…I mean…I don't." She fumbled. She did care. Why, she wasn't sure. "It's just surprising, that's all. Jason, at Serenity Hills?"

Sarah lifted an eyebrow. "He was visiting my grandmother."

"Visiting her?" Melanie couldn't hide the shock from her voice.

"More like, checking up on her. In a professional capacity," Sarah explained.

Now Melanie knew her eyes were bulging. "He made a house call? He actually cares?" She held up a hand. "That didn't come out right. But…seriously?"

Sarah shrugged. "He was there all right, and if you think that is shocking, what if I told you it wasn't the first time?"

Now Melanie was officially silenced. This made no sense. The Jason she knew was crisp and concise, didn't get to know his patients, and maybe didn't care to.

But there was another Jason, too, a softer, sweeter Jason. The Jason she'd grown up with. The Jason she'd seen the other night.

He had almost kissed her. She was sure of it!

And if he had? What then?

She didn't have time to think about that. Not now, not with the wedding only three days away. She'd think about it Sunday, when the festivities were over.

Only by Sunday Jason would be gone again. And it would be too late.

Chapter Twelve

Melanie didn't know why she was nervous. Abby had come to the shop last night as planned, and the dress had fit like a dream, and Melanie had finally slept through the night now that she knew it had. Chloe had left fifteen minutes before Abby's arrival, for her weekly yoga class (couldn't be late!), and after the gown was safely zipped into the dress bag and hung in the closet where they kept all their orders, including the pale pink bridesmaid dresses, she and Abby had even stopped by Jojo's for a glass of wine before calling it a night.

Everything should feel fine, really. But it didn't. Her stomach was fluttering and she felt a strange sense of apprehension as she looked out the window of her apartment while she adjusted the strap of her sling-back shoes.

Jason was picking her up for Abby's rehearsal dinner. It was no different than the hundreds of times they had gotten together over the years, or she'd stood by the window, looking for his car, ever since they were sixteen years old and he was driving his mom's oversized sedan that made parking a challenge for a new driver and sometimes required Melanie to hop out of the car and guide him in, both with words and larger than life hand gestures. They always laughed in relief when he'd succeeded.

She smiled now at the memory. One of a thousand. More than that, even. Tonight was just one to add to the mix.

But it was different, because the other night…That had been…awkward? Weird? Scary? Exciting? Downright confusing?

All of it and then some, she decided. And no doubt Jason was thinking the same. Or maybe not. It was hard to tell what Jason was thinking these days, what with that moment they shared and then Sarah's revelation.

A black SUV pulled up in front of her building and Melanie's heart sped up and she grabbed her clutch, locked the door behind her, and hurried down the stairs of the building.

Jason was wearing a navy suit and a striped tie, and he looked so handsome that she almost told him just that. And she would have, she always would have…before.

"Hey," she said as she slid into the seat beside him. She had managed to wiggle into her favorite navy dress, the one with the ruffle trim at the hem, and she'd paired it with strappy heels and a rose gold jewelry set that Beth had made, for the shop, yes, for brides, yes, but when Melanie had seen it, she'd known it had to be hers. And just like the flowers that brightened her kitchen table, she saw no reason to wait for special things for when she found "the one."

"You look nice," Jason said, giving her a friendly smile.

Nice. Yep. Nothing out of the ordinary. No weirdness there. He hadn't said she looked beautiful or anything. Hadn't lingered his gaze on her hips or lips or given any indication that he found her attractive in the romantic sense.

"Well, my diet is working. I think I'll stick with it a while."

She fastened her seatbelt as he merged into traffic. The drive to the club was short, and she could have accepted a ride with her parents and gone over earlier, but she didn't want to change her plans, and she had to admit that it was nice to show up with Jason at her side. Her go-to date. Her go-to person.

"Just don't go changing too much," he said, giving her a sidelong glance. His eyes crinkled at the corners when he grinned. "I like you just as you are."

Just as she was. She smiled, comforted by that, and leaned her head back, relaxing for the few minutes it would take before they arrived at the club. "I have a feeling my mother will be wound up tonight," she said.

This was her event, after all, her moment to shine. Because Abby's parents had passed away, her mother had asked Zach whether she should step in to help Abby with the wedding details, but she had two older sisters for that, and a soon-to-be-sister in law, Melanie thought with a grin.

"What has her anxious? Seeing one of her children get married?"

Melanie scoffed. "No, that part has her thrilled. Of course she'd love nothing more than to see *me* in a wedding dress."

"I think she wants nothing more than to see you be happy."

"I should probably let you know that my mother might...misread you being there with me tonight," Melanie said slowly. She skirted him a glance, trying to read his face. Was that a frown or amusement?

"Here I was worried she'd be disappointed you were showing up with me instead of a real date." He slowed to a stop at the traffic light and cocked a knowing eyebrow.

"Disappointed? Let's see. You're a doctor, for starters. And you get along with my family. And you're handsome—"

His face lit up. "You calling me handsome?"

She blinked, caught off-guard. Memories of that moment on the beach flooded back. "Now I'm going to feed your ego, and it's already quite inflated now that you're a hot shot ER doc."

He pinched his lips, but she could tell he was still

pleased. Thinking of what Sarah had said, she chewed on her lip, wondering if that last statement was even true. "My mother just wants me in a relationship. Whenever I see her, I sense this desperation in her eyes, like she's just waiting for me to tell her that I'm seeing someone."

"Well, I wouldn't want to mislead her. But if you must know, I think my mother will be misreading things tonight, too." Jason turned left at the corner. "The way she sees it, you're the perfect woman for me. Or maybe you're just perfect," he said after a beat, in a teasing tone.

Melanie stared at him a moment and then, catching his eye, looked away, out the window. They were nearly there.

"Well, it's hard to find a relationship in Oyster Bay," Melanie said. "So it makes sense that our mothers would think we were the obvious choice."

"Did you ever stop to think that maybe those relationships didn't work out because they weren't right for you?"

She considered this. "And who is right for me then?"

He gave a little smile. "Oh, someone you can be yourself with, someone who would never break up with you on Valentine's Day, and someone who wants the same things as you?"

He was describing someone she already knew. He was describing himself. Her heart began to beat a little faster as she looked at him, wondering if he was doing it on purpose or if he was merely saying that she should find someone that knew her. That got her. That…loved her.

But then she thought of the last thing he'd said. And she and Jason didn't want the same things at all, did they? He wanted to stay on in Boston, and she wanted to put down roots right here in Oyster Bay.

"What you're describing is hard to come by."

"Don't I know it," he said, blowing out a breath as he pulled up the drive of the country club and handed the keys to the valet driver.

"Do you think that's why you haven't dated anyone for long?" she asked as they walked up to the front doors and followed the sign to the Golfview Dining Room. But even though she'd asked, a part of her didn't want to know, didn't want to keep this conversation going anymore than she yearned to see it through. "Because they weren't right for you?"

He glanced at her, and she held her breath. "It's not easy to find a connection."

Her mouth felt dry. "Chemistry is a funny thing."

"And timing," he said, looking at her, his brown eyes rich, warm, and achingly familiar. She'd missed that face. "Timing changes everything. Sometimes one person is ready and the other is not. Sometimes, well." He gave a sad smile. "Sometimes the opportunity is lost. And then it wasn't meant to be."

"Or maybe it was," she said, not liking the defeatist tone in his voice. "And maybe someone just needs to fight for it. Take a chance."

His stare lingered for a long moment, and Melanie

didn't even realize that she was holding her breath until Abby jumped up in front of her and caused Melanie to jump.

"You scared me!"

She glanced at Jason, who seemed disappointed by the interruption, or maybe relieved, it was hard to tell. He gave the ladies a small bow. "I'll leave you to talk about wedding things. I see Zach over at the bar."

"Don't go scaring him off at the final hour," Abby warned, but she was smiling. Beaming, really. It was sweet to see how much love she had for Melanie's brother. It was all Melanie could have hoped for—for both of them. But as much as it touched her heart, it hurt a little bit too.

She wanted someone to smile about her like that. She was pretty sure that no one ever had.

Abby dropped into a nearby chair and blew out a breath. "No one ever warned me how exhausting this all was!"

"Didn't Bridget and Margo share their sisterly advice?" Melanie took a seat beside her, ignoring the place seating which was technically for one of her mother's oldest friends. She'd move soon, and she knew that her mother had done the seating charts for tonight and made sure to seat Melanie with Sarah and the Donovans. And Chloe. Her pulse sped up. She'd keep the conversation centered on Hannah's wedding plans.

Abby brushed a hand through the air. "Oh, you know me. I'm the youngest. I've been tuning those two out for

years. Maybe this was one time I should have listened."
She laughed, but despite the fatigue she claimed to feel,
she'd never looked more radiant.

She'd make a beautiful bride tomorrow.

"So we'll meet at the inn." Melanie felt the need to
confirm the plans they had agreed on, just in case
something needed to be changed last minute.

Abby nodded. "All the bridesmaids, too. But you'll be
there earlier with the dresses."

Melanie nodded. "I'll come over with Sarah."

Abby's eyes drifted around the room. The dress
seemed to finally be the least of her concerns, and
Melanie was relieved for that. "It's hard to imagine
tomorrow topping this party. Your parents hosted a
beautiful event for us."

Melanie had to agree. Her mother had put a lot of
thought into this dinner, from the menu to the
centerpieces to the thoughtful little photos that were
framed on each table, black and white pictures of Abby
and Zach over the years. She picked up the frame that
was in the center of the table they sat at now, smiling at
the fresh-faced teens that grinned back at her. It was
taken down at the beach; the lighthouse was barely visible
in the distance.

"I'm happy you guys ended up together," she said,
thinking of the years Abby and Zach had spent apart,
when Zach moved away from Oyster Bay.

"Some things are meant to be," Abby said simply.
"Deep down I always knew we would get back together."

"No you did not!" Melanie laughed, and Abby laughed too.

"You're right. I didn't. Not really. But I never found anyone else who could top him, either."

Melanie studied the photograph for a few more seconds and then set it back at the center of the table. She looked up, across the room, at the bar, to the one person who had never been topped in all these years either, and her heart did a little dance when she caught Jason's eye and he waved at her, and smiled a smile that she had just seen a few minutes ago, when Abby was talking about Zach.

*

Jason was the first to take a seat at the assigned table, near the front of the room, with a centerpiece made up of candles and a black and white photograph of Abby and Zach that must have been taken at Christmas. Abby's smile was radiant and Zach didn't look so bad himself. They were meant to be, Jason thought. Some things were.

And some things, unfortunately, were not.

He shifted in his chair as Melanie caught his eye and set a hand on Sarah's arm before she crossed the room. She seemed to glow tonight, and there was a confidence about her that hadn't been there in some time, maybe never. She was happy, and he wanted her to be happy, but was it selfish to want her to be happy with him?

"How's Sarah doing?" he asked as Melanie slid into the

seat beside him and unfolded her napkin.

"Disappointed that the speed dating was a bust. Talking about how she will end up in Serenity Hills one day." Melanie grinned. "The usual uplifting conversation."

Jason laughed. "Serenity Hills is a pretty swanky place."

Melanie's lips seemed to twitch, and she was giving him a funny look.

"Sarah said that you were visiting her grandmother there the other day."

He tried to pass his response off as casual, but she knew him too well. The knowing lift of her eyebrow didn't help any, either. "I thought it would be easier for me to check in on her at Serenity Hills."

"Twice?" Melanie clearly wasn't going to let this drop.

Right. So the girls had talked. He should have known she'd call him out on this. "My father made weekly visits there," he reminded her.

She leaned back in her chair, holding her glass of champagne. The smile on her face was pleased, maybe even a little satisfied.

He frowned. "What's that look for?"

"What look?" She widened her eyes, the picture of innocence, but she clearly caught on that he didn't find this matter to be funny. "I'm just saying that it's nice to see you following in your father's footsteps."

"I always have," he said, but he knew that wasn't exactly true. His father had supported his decision to go to Boston, to take the residency program, but his father had also always assumed he would come back, and for a while, Jason had too. "Well, maybe not always."

He gave her a small smile.

"Is it too much to hope that maybe you're happy to be back? That you're enjoying your time here?"

"Of course I'm enjoying my time here," he said. Their eyes locked, long enough for him to wonder if she knew, deep down, how he felt, if she'd ever known, but they were interrupted by the band kicking up, and the moment was broken. Seeing no point in trying to shout over the noise, he saw two options, to leave or to participate. And this was one time that he didn't want to leave.

"Want to dance?" he asked, tipping his head to the dance floor. Dinner would be served soon, but then they would be joined by the others. He needed to steal every moment alone with her while he still could.

His gut shifted when he thought of the weekend. The day after tomorrow he'd be back in Boston.

Melanie grinned. "Why not?" She set her champagne glass down on the table and they walked to the dance floor, where Jason immediately wondered why the hell he'd suggested this. He hadn't danced since high school, and even then, he'd never been good at it.

Fortunately, or perhaps not so fortunately, the song quickly shifted to something more manageable. Something slow, and romantic. "We could go—" he said at the same time she said, "I love this song."

She loved this song. He stopped, listening to it, not even recognizing it but deciding he liked it too, because what made Melanie happy made him happy, always had, always would.

"Okay then." He stepped forward, and spun her into a pirouette that made her laugh before bringing her closer to his chest, one hand holding hers, the other around her waist. Her hair was soft, brushing his cheek, and they said nothing as they swayed to the beat.

Halfway through the song, when he was already starting to dread its ending, when he would have to let go of her, when she would step back, walk away, maybe walk to the table where Sarah was now sitting, join in a conversation with the group, she stopped moving and looked him square in the eye.

"I wish you wouldn't leave," she said, simply, matter-of-factly, and even though she'd said as much before, asking him to come home, asking him to visit, telling him not to stay away so long the next time, she'd never said it like this.

He opened his mouth, wanting to tell her what she wanted to hear, but knowing that he couldn't. It wasn't enough. He'd settled for friends a long time ago because he wanted her in his life, and he still did, but this whole friend thing wasn't enough anymore. Maybe it never had been.

"And how would it be like if I stayed?" he asked.

She shrugged and started moving to the music again. "You tell me."

He sighed, deciding to go along with the game. Imagination. Daydreaming. Fantasy. "I suppose I'd take over my father's practice, and my mother would be happy. My father too," he said, feeling his jaw tighten at the thought. The clinic would stay open. He'd see patients with minor ailments, he'd rarely save lives, but he might still make a difference in one or two. He might be remembered, not forgotten, or worse, never known.

"I'd be happy, too," she told him, smiling so bright that it took everything in him not to lean down and kiss her, to feel that warmth, that love, and to never let it go. "And you and I would come to all our friends' weddings. And rehearsal dinners. And we'd always be each other's plus ones. And we'd never have to be alone again. We'd just go on and on like this, like we always have. You and me."

He was looking her in the eye, his breath felt ragged, and she blinked at him, her smile slipping for one, tentative moment before returning again, a little less bright, a little more hopeful.

"You and me. Sounds perfect."

Perfect, he thought, as the music stopped and she stepped away, smiling over her shoulder as she returned to the table, fell into conversation with Sarah, laughed at something her friend said.

It did sound perfect.

Chapter Thirteen

Chloe was already in the shop when Melanie arrived at Bayside Brides the next morning. Her shift would be short, and she and Sarah were scheduled to meet at the Harper House Inn at noon to go over last-minute details before the rest of the wedding party joined for a light lunch, followed by hair and makeup before the ceremony at five. Out of town guests were staying at both the inn and the Oyster Bay Hotel in town, and Bridget had assured Abby that her husband Jack would be taking care of all the guests today, so that her attention wouldn't be divided.

Melanie would be bringing all the bridesmaids and flower girl dresses with her, along with the wedding dress and tulle veil that Abby had originally chosen. Because she knew that she wouldn't lose the knot in her stomach until she had everything off her hands and every dress fit and every woman was happy, she went right to the walk-in closet near the dressing rooms that they used to store the dresses that were already purchased and waiting for pick-up. She scrutinized each one through their dress bags.

"So it's all finished then?"

Melanie hadn't heard Chloe come into the closet and she set a hand to her chest, waiting for her heart to resume a normal speed. "You scared me."

"I'm not that bad," Chloe said, and there was a softness in her expression that told Melanie she was referring to more than just startling her. She walked over to Abby's wedding gown that was covered in a breathable plastic lining and studied it. "This is beautiful, Melanie. Really."

Melanie looked at her cousin in surprise. "Thank you. I worked really hard on it."

"I know," Chloe said. "You enjoyed making it, too. I haven't seen you that excited about something since…well, if you don't mind me saying this, since Doug."

Melanie lifted an eyebrow. Chloe made a good point with that comment, even if she struck a nerve. "I have been excited about making this dress," she said, and she wasn't going to deny it, not to Chloe, not to herself. And Chloe was right: it was good to be passionate about something other than her romantic future. "I'm sorry if it got in the way of other things. That wasn't my intention. That's not how I wanted it to be."

Chloe nodded. "I know. And I also know that it wouldn't be that way always. We just have to reorganize."

Melanie frowned at her. "You mean…"

"I looked at the spreadsheet you gave me, and I have to admit that you made a strong case." Chloe gave her a small smile. "You forced my hand, and I think I needed that. It's easy to get stuck in a rut sometimes. There's something comforting about staying put rather than trying to move forward."

Melanie didn't need to hear that twice. It was what she'd done for the past year, after all, hiding in her apartment, and it was what she'd done long before that, when she'd set aside her passions, and somewhere along the way, forgotten about them.

"You look good, by the way," Chloe remarked.

"Thanks. It's this new diet I'm trying." She could only hope this meant she might slip into her bridesmaid dress without the aid of control top undergarments.

"Not just that," Chloe said. "You seem…happier. You have a glow about you, and something tells me it's not just because you pulled off this stunning dress."

"I am happier," Melanie realized.

"New guy in your life?" Chloe asked.

"Not a new guy, no. More like…an old guy. It's been nice having Jason back in town." She hated the thought of him leaving again tomorrow. Who knew how long he would stay away the next time. Sure, he had mentioned the summer, but things always seemed to pop up and keep him away. "He was the one who got me out of this rut."

"Pep talk?"

Melanie thought about this for a moment. "More just by being him, I suppose."

"Some people have a way of bringing out our best selves," Chloe said as she began removing the bridesmaid dresses from the hooks. She gave Melanie a funny smile. "You sort of have that effect on me."

"Me? But my life is…a mess." Melanie laughed. It wasn't true, not as of late, but hadn't Chloe seen how things had gone for the past year? It wasn't her shining moment, that was for certain.

"You have dreams, and aspirations, and sure, sometimes they're misdirected, but you still reach for them. That takes courage. And I, well, I admire that."

Melanie leaned in to give her cousin a quick hug but stepped back when she remembered that she was holding two of the bridesmaid dresses, including her own. "Wouldn't want to wrinkle these."

Chloe's eyes were wide. "Um, no. And we definitely don't have time to do any last-minute alterations." She checked her watch. "I have an appointment any minute."

"So I'll see you tonight then, at the ceremony?"

Chloe grinned. "Wouldn't miss it."

*

Melanie's step was officially lighter as she finished loading the dresses into the back of her car. After putting down the back row of seats, she could lay them all flat, making sure that the most important dress, Abby's dress, was set on top. Sarah was helping a last-minute customer, but they'd have to be on their way soon. Abby was probably staring out the window, anticipating the arrival of her wedding dress.

The thought of it gave Melanie goose bumps. Every time.

She locked the car and walked over toward Angie's, deciding some caffeine was in order before she exchanged her work clothes for bridal wear, when she saw him, up ahead, walking right toward her. Doug.

She hesitated, and then decided she had no choice but to keep moving forward, even if their paths would cross. It was unavoidable.

He gave her a slow smile as he approached, and his eyes raked over her, just once, but in an obvious enough way that she couldn't help but smooth her skirt out of sudden awareness that she was wearing one.

"Melanie." He came to a full stop, catching her by surprise. She'd assumed there would be a polite hello, followed by a quickening of pace.

"Doug!" She forced a bright, cheerful grin, even if she felt nothing of the sort. She felt on edge and uncomfortable, like the air had been popped from her balloon.

He gave her a slow smile, the kind that used to make her heart speed up and go all giddy, but that didn't happen this time. "You look really nice. Really good, actually."

Was that surprise in his tone? "Thank you," she said simply. She waited for the flutter, the heart-soaring reaction to a compliment like this, because this was what she'd wanted, wasn't it, for Doug to still find her appealing?

But it wasn't what she wanted, she realized. Not anymore.

"You're going to be at the wedding tonight?"

She frowned at him. Deeply. Was this the kind of conversation they used to have back when they were dating, or was he just nervous? "It's my brother's wedding."

"Oh." He laughed. "Of course. I was thinking of Abby…"

Melanie shifted the weight on her feet. More like he hadn't been thinking of her at all, of the fact that not only was she going to be at the wedding, but that she was in it. That he had accepted an invitation to a family event—her family's event—without giving her any consideration at all. Unbelievable.

"I'm sorry, is there something you needed?" It was wedding day, the busiest day there could be, and nothing was going to make things go off-plan for her today, not even a surprise conversation with her ex-boyfriend, who hadn't exchanged words with her in over a year.

"I was hoping we could talk. Before tonight. Maybe have a coffee? Just for a few minutes?" He thrust his hands into his pockets, and she realized for the first time that he actually did seem a little nervous, that maybe he was even squirming a little.

This did make her smile.

"It won't take long," he insisted.

Still not completely convinced, Melanie checked her watch. She really didn't have extra time, not today, but she also didn't know what Doug wanted to say, and a year ago, even six months ago (okay, even three months ago) she would have only dreamed of this moment. "I have about fifteen minutes."

His smile was one of relief. "Okay, great. We can grab something from Angie's, if you want?"

Even though she had been on her way to that exact spot to get a coffee, she had lost her taste for it. It felt too official, too formal, like he was going to break some huge news to her or something.

Oh, Lord. Was Doug *engaged* to Jessica? She blinked as she tried to process this possibility. Perhaps he was. She wasn't as up to date on his comings and goings as Sarah or Jason might think.

"Why don't we take a walk to the town square?" She could use the air, and it would be a lot less awkward than sitting across the table from him.

Besides, it was right around the corner from her car, making for an easy getaway should the need arise.

They walked the two and a half blocks in silence, finally settling on a park bench under a maple tree, a few yards from the sidewalk.

"So," she said, a little breathlessly. "You want to talk."

What would she say, when he told her he was getting married, that he wanted her to be the first to know? Would she be able to be civil, wish him well, or would she be insulted, furious that he thought she still cared?

Because…she didn't care, she realized. At least, not in the way she had before. She looked at Doug, her eyes roaming his face, and for the first time in so long, she realized that she actually didn't care at all. She didn't care that he was coming to the wedding. She didn't care that he was dating Jessica. She didn't care if he decided to propose to her, even. She didn't care what he had to say. She didn't even find him all that attractive anymore. How could anyone who was this self-centered be remotely attractive?

"I just wanted to be sure that it would be okay between us, with me being there tonight. With Jessica."

"That's thoughtful of you, Doug," she said, tipping her head. He didn't seem to pick up on the condescending tone of her voice.

He gave a cocky grin. "I try."

"Do you?" She smiled, a big, broad, confident smile. "You didn't try last year, when you ended our relationship on Valentine's Day," she pointed out. He blinked, seeming surprised at her honesty, and opened his mouth.

But she wasn't finished yet. "I assume that Jessica convinced you to talk to me, considering that I am the sister of the groom and all and that I co-own Bayside Brides, and that she does the invitations for oh, ninety-eight percent of our clientele?"

There was defiance in Doug's eyes. His jaw was set, and he lifted it a notch. "She suggested I smooth things over…"

Melanie nodded, gave him a little wince. "Right. Of course she did." She gathered up her handbag and stood to leave. "The thing is, though, Doug, I don't care."

He frowned. "What do you mean, you don't care?"

"I mean that I wasted enough of my time caring about someone who didn't care about me."

"Now that's not fair!" Doug said gruffly. He rose to stand next to her, but she was already starting to walk away. "Melanie. Wait."

She should have kept walking, kept moving forward the way she wanted to, the way that she had been doing, the way that was bringing joy to her life again. But she didn't like unfinished business any more than she liked the person she used to be. The person she had been, when she was with him.

She turned, and she realized that she was smiling, overcome with a feeling that she hadn't felt in so long, she barely even recognized it. Pride. Satisfaction. Fulfillment. She didn't need Doug. Looking back, she never had.

"No, Doug. I've done enough waiting. Have a nice

time at the wedding. I'm sure I'll see you there, of course. But don't try to talk to me again, Doug. We have nothing left to say to each other."

"Nothing left to say to each other! But we dated—"

"Yes, we dated, and you treated me appallingly, and I allowed you to. And now I am saying good-bye, Doug."

She turned, suppressing the urge to burst out in cheer, her spirits lifting further when she saw Jason across the street. She waved, hurrying her pace, but he didn't wave back; in fact, he looked downright angry as he turned and walked away, without even looking back.

*

Time to go, Jason thought, as he power walked up Main Street toward the clinic. This was it, his last day here. Any doubt, any hope, had been erased.

And he had been hoping, he realized, as he stopped in front of the big Victorian house with the sign out front that had been there for as long as he'd been on this earth. He'd been hoping that there would be a reason to stay, a reason big enough to turn down that fantastic opportunity in Boston, a reason to know that he would have no regrets and that his choice was one made with his whole heart, and head.

He walked up the steps and fished the keys from his pocket. He didn't know why he was here. He'd closed out his cases. Tomorrow he'd be on his way back to Boston, to his apartment, his job, his life.

The lobby was empty and dim. The only light filtered through the blinds, and the fish even seemed to be asleep. He looked around the room for a purpose, but the magazines were straightened, the lollipop jar filled, even the plant on the corner of the reception desk looked like it had been watered, although who was he to know? He took care of people, not plants. Or maybe, he just took care of people's bodies. His father, his father was the one who took care of the whole person.

With a heavy tread, Jason walked back, past the receptionist desk, and turned back for one good look at the room. If he closed his eyes he could still picture himself sitting in that far corner, with Melanie and her ripped up bear. He had all the confidence in the world that his father would make everything okay. Everyone in town had that confidence. What would they have now?

He soaked it all in, committing it to memory: the lollipops, the coat hook for adults, the smaller one for children, the fish tank in the corner, and the stacks of children's books that his mother collected over the years. Every inch of this place had been designed with intention and care. And now, now it was time to say good-bye. To move on. Maybe that was the natural order of things.

With a sad smile he walked to the door, turning only at the sound of something rustling.

"Jason?" His father was standing outside exam room one, a quizzical smile on his face. "I thought that was you. What brings you by?"

Jason shrugged and stuffed his hands into his pockets.

"Just taking one last look at it, I suppose."

His father's expression didn't flinch. "It's a good place. Not as exciting as the emergency room in the big city, of course, but I've been happy here. Satisfied."

"And you're sure?" Jason asked. He had to try, at least once. He didn't want his father to have any regrets.

Or maybe, the person he should be worried about was himself.

"As sure as you are about going back to Boston," his father replied.

Touché. With that one statement he'd managed to hit Jason the hardest, to tap into his insecurities and doubts and fears, damn it. Jason walked farther into the room. Up close in this light his father looked worn out and tired, the impact of his health more evident.

"The thing is that I'm not so sure at all," he admitted.

His father's mouth crooked into a smile. "Can I admit something? I'm not so sure I'm ready to retire, either. I will, I have to, for my health, and for your mother," his father stressed, making it clear that despite his words, his decision had been made. "But it won't be easy on me. Even though I knew this day would come, eventually, it's harder than I thought it would be."

Jason nodded. "I understand." Leaving Oyster Bay this time felt permanent.

His father rolled back on his heels, soaked in the room, and then shifted his eyes back to Jason, where they stayed. "I hope a month is enough time to find a replacement. After that, I'll have to list the building for sale."

Of course. The building was beautiful; it could be used for any purpose, really. A law firm. A small inn. Maybe even someone's home. The entire upstairs was empty, used for storage. Once there had been talk of expanding, putting in more exam rooms, adding to the staff. But then, all that talk eventually faded away.

Right around the time that Jason decided to do his residency in Boston, he realized.

"You know I would never pressure you to come back and take over," his father said gruffly. "But I want you to know the invitation is always there, if you want to, that is."

Jason's mouth felt dry. He didn't want the clinic to close, but to give up Boston, everything he was doing there?

"Take your time," his father said, giving him a pat on the shoulder. "This kind of life, it's not exciting, but it's meaningful. It's not for everyone."

Jason nodded. He hadn't had a heart to heart like this in too long. It was easier, sometimes, to keep everything bottled up, to push desires and emotions aside. It was what he'd been trained to do. Just keep going. Moving. Acting. Doing what his head knew was best. But his head didn't know anymore. And his heart… His heart was in Oyster Bay. It always had been.

Chapter Fourteen

The Harper House Inn wasn't hosting the wedding, but Melanie decided that it may as well have. There were bunches of white balloons tied to the front porch posts and the entire lobby was electric with excitement. Bridget's daughter Emma came bounding to the front door to greet them, her hair in pink foam curlers.

"Are those the dresses? Is my dress in there?"

"It sure is," Melanie said, patting the dress bags that were draped over her arm, which was starting to ache from the weight. "Which room does your mom want us in?"

"Room two," Emma said primly, leading them to the stairs, where she then sprinted up them at full speed.

Melanie looked over her shoulder and shared a laugh with Sarah. "I think someone is excited."

"Even I'm excited. And I shouldn't be. I'm going to this wedding alone. Again."

Melanie didn't know whether or not to mention that she might be attending the wedding alone, too. She'd texted Jason after she went back to the shop to meet Sarah, thinking that maybe she'd misread things, that maybe he hadn't seen her, but in her heart she knew that wasn't true. He'd seen her talking to Doug, and he'd assumed something that wasn't there. Assumed that she was still hung up on a guy who was no good and never had been.

She needed to set him straight. Today. Before it was too late.

Abby was already in the guest suite with Margo and Bridget, all of them wearing the white fluffy robes that Bridget supplied for the inn. On the pedestal table near the window was a three-tiered silver tray of finger sandwiches, and a bowl of sliced fruit, but no one was eating.

"I'm not late, am I?" Melanie asked, worriedly. She and Sarah immediately began hanging up the dresses in the empty closet, except Abby's dress. Abby's dress was hung on the hook on the back of the door, on full display, where everyone could see it.

"You're fine. They're all early. We couldn't wait!" Abby seemed to glow as she popped a bottle of champagne, eliciting a peal of delight from Emma. Oh, to be nine again, Melanie thought.

"I don't even think Emma was this excited for my

wedding," Bridget said, shaking her head. She began removing the curlers from her daughter's hair.

"I've become quite an expert at being a flower girl," Emma said solemnly. "You can't just dump all the flowers at once. You have to spread them out, make them last the entire length of the aisle."

All the women nodded in response. "Yes, Emma. Exactly."

Melanie winked at Abby. "So we're just waiting on Hannah and Evie?"

"And Kelly," Abby said. Of course, even though she wasn't related to the Harper sisters, they'd taken her in like family, and she had been fitted for a bridesmaid dress, too. "And your mother."

Her mother. Of course. Melanie's mother had been given the choice of getting ready with the guys or joining the women at the inn, and of course she'd chosen the latter. Melanie knew she should support her mother, she knew that she should share in her mother's excitement for the day, but she couldn't shake the apprehension she felt ever since Jason's reaction today.

She checked her phone, hoping to see a response to her text, or a missed phone call. But there was nothing.

She chewed her bottom lip. He wouldn't stand her up. Jason never stood her up. Jason was dependable. Reliable. The one person she could always trust.

The one.

She blinked. No. She couldn't think that way, even if a

part of her, a part that had pushed past the confusion and the dreams and the ideal image she had of how life should be, wanted to think just that way.

"I want to try on my dress!" Emma begged.

"We should wait for the others," Margo said, but her expression looked like it needed some convincing.

"We do have a couple hours," Sarah said. "Hair and makeup should happen first."

"But please let's leave some room for last-minute alterations," Melanie said. The last thing she needed was to be stitching up a ripped seam as the bride was about to go down the aisle.

"And we should eat first," warned Bridget.

"Oh, who can eat on a day like this? It's my wedding day!" Abby's eyes shone with joy as she walked over to gaze at her dress.

There was a pounding on the stairs and everyone straightened with excitement. "They're here!" Emma cried, as the Donovan sisters appeared in the doorway, Kelly in tow, and Melanie's mother right behind, holding her navy dress by a hanger. Immediately the sisters ran to the wedding dress, to admire it with Abby.

"Hi, Mom," Melanie said, leaning in to give her a hug by way of greeting.

"What's wrong?" her mother whispered. "You look stressed."

Did she look stressed? Weddings were stressful, after all. Only today it wasn't the wedding that was bothering her. And her mother no doubt knew it.

"I'm fine," she said brightly, even though nothing could be further from the truth. Tomorrow Jason was leaving. And she didn't know on what terms he would go. She wasn't sure which thought was worse, actually. That he was leaving. That he wasn't coming back. Or that something seemed to have shifted between them.

"Actually, I'm the one that's stressed," Karen said, pulling back, and sure enough, Melanie could see the panic in her eyes. Her first child was getting married today, and while Melanie didn't have firsthand experience as a mother, she'd dealt with enough of them at the store to know just how overwhelming and emotional it could be.

"Oh, that's right. I forgot about your seam." She winked at her mother when she started to protest. "Bridget? Is there another room we can use for a few minutes so I can work on the mother of the groom's dress? Small hem issue. Won't take more than a minute or two."

Bridget looked up from the bed, where she was gathered with the other bridesmaids, everyone now holding a glass of Champagne. "Room three is free right now. They aren't checking in until two." She glanced at Abby and explained, "Zach's old coworker and his wife."

Of course, with the entire inn being filled exclusively with wedding guests this weekend, they would be forgiving, but Melanie would still be careful not to do anything that would create more work for Bridget or her husband today. This was a family wedding for all of them.

Melanie gathered her mother's dress from her arms and led her down the hall to the next door. It was a beautiful house, a Victorian by the sea, and even though it was miles from town, something about the architecture reminded her of Dr. Sawyer's clinic and his decision to retire. She hated harboring a secret that no one else shared. Other than Jason, of course.

"You didn't need to pull me out of the room," Karen tutted once they were behind closed doors.

Melanie shrugged as she set the dress bag on the bed. "They could use a few minutes as their own family for a moment. We are the in-laws, after all."

Karen's eyes went wide. "Scary thought. When I think of my own mother-in-law…" They both laughed. Over the years Karen and Grandma Dillon had become friends, but it hadn't started out that way. Sure, Grandma Dillon hadn't worn white to her parents' wedding the way some mothers of the groom tried to do at Bayside Brides, but she had made a tearful display during the ceremony, apparently howling like it was a funeral rather than a celebration.

"You're allowed to cry, you know," Melanie told her mother now. Not in the wailing sense of Grandma Dillon, but that went without saying. To most.

"It's a happy day," her mother said with a sigh. "I love Abby and she's been like a part of the family since she was a teenager. Sort of like Jason."

And there it was, of course. Only instead of telling her

mother that she and Jason were just friends, only friends, and would only ever be friends, now Melanie felt like there was a different protest to make, a different excuse for why they weren't together and maybe never would be.

"That's a beautiful dress you made for Abby," her mother said, breaking the silence. "It caught my eye the moment I walked in. Maybe you can make your own dress one day. When you…"

Melanie stifled a sigh. "Maybe." It was the one wedding she hadn't planned, but she knew her mother already had ideas.

"I know you would like nothing more than to see me married," she said, feeling a little defensive.

"I want nothing more than to see you *happy*," her mother stressed. "You were the one who always wanted to be in a relationship, and if that's what you wanted, then I wanted it for you."

Melanie thought about this for a moment and then dropped onto the bed. She would smooth the duvet before she went back to join the others. "I wasted a lot of time on jerks."

"There are nice men out there, Melanie." Her mother came to sit beside her. "Jason Sawyer has always been a nice man."

"Jason is going back to Boston tomorrow, Mom." Melanie eyed her mother sidelong.

Oddly, her mother didn't seem fazed by that comment. "Life has a way of working out the way it's supposed to."

Melanie looked out the window that had a view of the Atlantic that seemed to go for as long as the eye could see. When she was little, her mother used to tell her all sorts of things to make her feel better, like that Santa would still find them the one time they went to visit Grandma and Grandpa Dillon for Christmas, or that she would indeed go to prom, and love every minute of it.

And she had. Thanks to Jason.

Today, just like then, she hoped her mother was right. And because she had faith, and hope, and because it was wedding day, when magical things happened, she dared to believe it.

*

Jason shrugged into his suit coat. He checked the clock on his bedside table—digital, a relic from another time, even though in many ways it felt like no time had passed at all since he was the lanky teenage kid who used to slam down on it every morning when the alarm went off for school.

He was supposed to meet Melanie at the Botanic Garden; she'd be travelling with the wedding party, all the women in one limo, Zach's side coming over from the Oyster Bay Hotel.

Jason's parents were invited, they all had come, the Dillons and the Sawyers weren't just neighbors, but family. They'd shared a few Thanksgiving dinners together when relatives couldn't make it into town. They'd spent Super Bowl Sundays together and Memorial

Day cookouts. And now they would share Zach's wedding day.

How would it be for Melanie's wedding day? How would it be for his own?

He didn't like thinking about it, and he didn't have time to, either. He hurried down the stairs and into the kitchen, expecting to find both of his parents but instead just finding his mother. She was wearing a dark purple dress and her grandmother's pearls, and a smile that made Jason uneasy.

"Your father will be right down. He spilled some coffee on his shirt."

"You let him have coffee?" Jason frowned. For the entire two weeks he had been home, his mother had forbidden his father from touching it.

She tossed up her hands. "He's going to do what he's going to do. Just like you're going to do what you're going to do. And I have to accept that."

Something told Jason that they weren't talking about coffee anymore. "I saw Dad this morning, at the clinic."

She frowned. "He was at the clinic? He told me he was going into town to get some exercise. Moderate, of course."

Jason gave a little smile. "Moderate. Of course." He heaved a sigh. His mother's delivery wasn't always on point, but her heart was in the right place. It was in a better place than his had been, for a long time. "I only stopped by the clinic for a minute."

"Forgot something?" Her eyes were sharp.

Jason pulled in a breath. It would be so much easier to use that excuse, but he didn't have it in him. He felt weary and out of sorts and depressed as hell, if he was being honest with himself. When he'd first arrived back in Oyster Bay, he was counting down the days until he went back to Boston, but now he would be leaving tomorrow and the thought had lost its luster.

"I guess I wanted to take one last look. It's difficult to think of Dad retiring."

"It is," his mother said, her tone softening along with her expression. She gave a sad smile. "I still remember the day your father bought that old house. We wallpapered that lobby ourselves, you know. Just the two of us. The entire future seemed so big and bright at the time. We've shared a lot together."

Jason tried to imagine his parents young and excited and felt a pull in his chest. "That's nice to think about. You and Dad. Young, happy."

"Oh, we're still happy," his mother said airily. She gave him a cheeky smile as she bent down to slip on her shoes. "Just not too young, I'm afraid."

"You still have a lot of years ahead of you," he said gruffly. "Dad's heart attack is bringing out a morbid streak in you."

"Quite the opposite," his mother jerked her head up in surprise. "It's made us realize how much life we have left to live and think about how we want to spend it. It's time for the next phase. And just the like the last one, we'll be enjoying it together."

"That sounds nice," Jason said.

"Traveling? Or retiring?"

"Having someone to share those phases with, I meant." Tomorrow at this time he'd be in his studio apartment in the Back Bay, alone, with the television for company and probably some takeout from the Chinese place on the corner for dinner.

And Melanie…Well, there was no sense in thinking of Melanie, was there?

"You've had someone special to share life's ups and downs with. Melanie has always been a constant force in your life." His mother gave him a knowing look. "Those kinds of relationships are special, Jason."

Didn't he know it? "I'm not her type," he said simply. "Melanie prefers jocks and players, always has."

"And you know this because…" His mother's smile was one of amusement. Honestly, she was exasperating at times like this.

"Because she's probably back together with Doug McKinney." Of all people. He'd break her heart again, of course he would, and this time, Jason wouldn't be there to pick up the pieces.

But of course, he would. Because he could never turn his back on Melanie. And that was just the problem.

"So the only reason that you and Melanie are not together is because she prefers jocks and players and because she may or may not be back together with Doug

McKinney?"

Jason nodded. "That's correct."

"And nowhere in that list of excuses did you mention that you and Melanie are only friends and that is the only way you see her." Her smile was sly. "Interesting."

"Mom," Jason groaned, but he was fighting off a smile too. One that didn't match the heaviness in his heart. "It doesn't matter now."

"It absolutely does matter!" Her tone was sharp, jarring him. "Haven't you learned anything from your father?"

"I learned to be a doctor!" Jason frowned, squaring his shoulders with indignation.

His mother shook her head, walked over, and patted him on the shoulder. "Sometimes in life, Jason, you have to follow your heart. You have to take a risk. And you have to follow it. Opportunities are all around, but the ones that matter the most won't be there forever."

Jason gave his mother a small smile. Damn it if she wasn't always right.

"What did I miss?" his father said gruffly as he walked back into the room, adjusting his tie.

"Only that Jason has finally admitted that he is in love with Melanie," his mother said lightly.

"About damn time!" his father boomed. "Now, does she know it yet?"

No, Jason thought, as they walked to the car together. But she would. Tonight. She would finally know.

Chapter Fifteen

Jason scanned the tent of the reception, looking for a woman in a pink-colored bridesmaid dress, the same woman he had watched all through the ceremony, instead of the bride, the same woman he had watched grow from a young girl with two braids in her hair. He knew her laughter, he knew her fears, but there was one thing that he didn't know. He didn't know how she felt about him, not truly, not deep down, and that was scary as hell.

"Jason!"

He turned at his name. A woman in a bridesmaid dress, all right, but not the brunette he was hoping for. It was Sarah, with her blond hair pulled up in some kind of knot, her eyes bright, and her smile kind. Jason could understand why Melanie was friends with her. She was a good fit to Oyster Bay, and he hoped she would stay.

"Sarah." He grinned and walked over to her. "You look nice this evening."

She blushed as she looked at the ground. "Try telling that to a few of the eligible men in town, if you don't mind."

"I don't mind," he said. "But I'm sure they've noticed all on their own."

She gave him a look that showed she wasn't buying his words. "If they noticed, then why didn't they do something about it? Ask me to dinner…strike up a conversation?" She blew out a sigh.

"Maybe they're nervous." Jason shrugged. "It's not as easy for us guys as you seem to think it is."

She peered at him. "Are you speaking from firsthand experience?"

Ah. Caught. He shrugged. He liked Sarah, felt an easy connection with her. The connection was, of course, Melanie.

At his lack of response, Sarah's lips twisted into a sly smile. "Well, if you are holding back feelings from someone, I think it would behoove you to share those feelings."

He studied her carefully, wondering if she knew something he didn't, or if she was hinting about herself. His pulse kicked up a notch. The last thing he wanted to do was mislead her.

"Advice noted," he said, rolling back on his heels.

"I have to go gather up the bouquets and set them on the cake table," Sarah explained. "But before I rush off, I wanted to thank you again for your help with my grandmother. This isn't easy. She isn't easy. But, well, you've made all this much smoother than it would have been without you here."

Jason was about to say that she would have been in just as good of hands with his father, if not better, until he remembered again that his father was retiring. It still didn't seem real.

"You're a good doctor, Jason. I just wanted to thank you for going above and beyond. Not everyone is as invested as you are, you know."

"My father's the one to credit," he said, shaking off the compliment. He wasn't used to them, and he certainly didn't feel that he deserved any special praise. He was just doing his job, but something told him that saying that wasn't what Sarah wanted to hear, and maybe it wasn't the truth either.

In Boston, he did a job. Here in Oyster Bay…it was more of a calling, wasn't it?

"Well, clearly the apple doesn't fall from the tree," Sarah said. She looked around the room, waving at Bridget and Margo who were waiting for her near the cake. She slid him a glance. "Duty calls."

"Have fun."

"I intend to," she said with a smile. She hesitated as she lifted up a corner of her dress. "And Jason? If I may be so bold as to help you the way you have helped me? Melanie is near the gazebo, just finishing up the groom's side family photos."

Jason opened his mouth to protest but the look on Sarah's face told him it was no use.

And that left him with no excuse, did it?

*

Melanie stepped down from the gazebo and watched with a happy sigh as Abby and Zach walked into the tent on the back lawn where the reception was being held, Abby's veil floating in the breeze that blew in off the ocean. The wedding had been wonderful, and not just because the weather had held up. There was joy in the air today, genuine heartfelt love, from the moment Chip walked the last of his nieces down the aisle to the point where Zach took her hand. There had been readings, carefully selected by Abby and presented by her sisters, and there was music from the string quartet that sat just to the side of the groomsmen. And oh, there were flowers. So many flowers. And the tulips had chosen this weekend to bloom.

Melanie knew many clients who had married at the Botanic Garden, but she could firmly say that none had looked as pretty as Abby.

"She's a beautiful bride," she said wistfully to her mother, who stood at her side, letting the happy couple steal a few moments to themselves. Soon there would be speeches and dinner and dancing and the cutting of the cake. And all too soon, it would be over. The dress would be cleaned and packed up, tucked away as a memory, or perhaps passed on to the daughter that Abby and Zach might someday have. Their future was open, full of possibility, but certain in so many ways.

The dress couldn't have come out better if she'd had two months to make it instead of two weeks. It was everything that Abby had been searching for and couldn't find, and it fit her perfectly.

But it wasn't just her handiwork that had made the dress look so beautiful, Melanie knew. It was Abby's happiness. It had been the perfect wedding, just as she dreamed it would be.

Her mother turned and gave her a smile. "You will be a beautiful bride, too, someday."

"Mother!" Melanie gave her a warning look. "I thought we talked about this." But it seemed her mother was still hell-bent on seeing her settled down, the old-fashioned way.

"If you *want* to," her mother protested. She skirted her eyes to the right as she took Melanie's father's arm. "And something tells me you will."

Melanie frowned, not knowing where her mother was going with this, and looked to the corner of the garden, under the trellis, where Jason was standing, his hands in his suit pockets, a strange smile on his face. One that didn't exactly scream happiness. More like wariness.

She huffed out a breath and turned to watch as her entire family disappeared into the building. No escape now. She was alone with Jason, in a beautiful English garden, and somehow, she'd never felt more out of place.

"I saw you earlier," she said as he approached. "I can explain."

He shook his head. "You don't need to explain anything to me."

"But I do," she said, frowning at his reaction. Didn't he care? If she was with Doug? If she wasn't? Maybe she'd had it all wrong.

"No," he said, giving her a small smile. "Because it doesn't change a damn thing, Melanie Dillon."

She stared at him, maybe glared at him. "What is that supposed to mean? What happened to my best friend who has my absolute best interest at heart at all times?"

Jason gave a little shrug, but his eyes locked on hers, holding them tightly. "He went and fell in love with you."

Melanie stared at him, at the man she had watched grow from a little boy to a successful doctor, to the man who had always been there, always would be, if she'd let him. "But—"

He shook his head, his smile turning a little sad. "But nothing. It's just what it is, Mel. You're the one. My best friend. My oldest friend. My everything. And I couldn't wait one more day without telling you that."

"Because you're going back to Boston tomorrow," she said, swallowing hard.

"Not because I'm going back to Boston. Because I've been holding it in for over fifteen years and I couldn't hold it in even one more day." He was looking at her, his expression hopeful, but slightly resigned. "You don't need to say anything, Mel. But you're right about one thing. I *do* care. I will always care. Tomorrow, I will still care. And we've always told each other everything. And so this is something you needed to know."

Melanie swallowed the lump that was building in her throat. Fifteen years? Did he mean?

"Prom." She blinked, and a single hot tear slipped down her cheek.

He shook his head. "Happiest day of my life. Went to prom with the girl of my dreams."

The girl of his dreams. Her mind was spinning. A hundred memories raced through her thoughts. A hundred memories that now felt different. Sweeter.

"But you went away," she said. He'd gone away. Stayed away.

"Self-preservation, I suppose." He pulled in a breath. "Couldn't sit around watching you get all swoony over guys like Doug McKinney every day, now, could I?"

Doug. "What happened with Doug wasn't what you thought." She had so much she had to tell him. So much she needed to say. "Doug was never the one for me. Neither were any of the others before him."

Jason's jaw set as the silence filled the space between them. This was the moment, she knew, that everything they'd shared had been leading to. And in that moment, he looked different, weathered, older, wiser, not like the guy who could make her laugh or dry her tears, but like a man she needed to take seriously.

They didn't make a lot of men like Jason, did they? If they did, she'd never found another. Never would. Never could.

"There is one thing I haven't told you either," she said, letting out a shaky breath.

His gaze was stern, his lips a thin line. He was waiting for what she would say next. And oh, she couldn't wait to say it. Out loud. For all the world to hear.

"You're the one, Jason. You always were. I just didn't know it."

"Sure took you long enough to figure it out," he said, brushing a loose strand from her updo as the breeze picked up. His face broke out into a grin as he reached forward and slid his arms around her waist. It was the same embrace they'd always shared, casually, without enough thought or care before.

"I had a lot of things to figure out," she said, holding him a little tighter. "What about Boston?"

His eyes shone with amusement. "What about it?"

She swatted his shoulder. "Your job. It's what you always wanted."

"*You're* what I always wanted," he said, leaning in to press his nose against hers. "Besides, I can't let that clinic be sold off to a random stranger, can I?"

"You mean?" Her eyes filled with tears again, and this time she knew there would be no blinking them away.

"I'm home, Mel. I'm right where I belong."

And then, he kissed her.

Epilogue

Four weeks later, the retired Dr. Sawyer and his wife embarked for a European vacation for an undisclosed amount of time, though Jason was of the opinion they would never miss a summer in Oyster Bay.

He and Melanie were spending the Saturday sprucing up the clinic before he officially took over on Monday morning. Of course, he'd already made two house calls this morning, one to Serenity Hills to check on Esther Preston, who had invited him to a romantic dinner this evening, to which he'd respectfully declined, and another to Bridget Harper, who had slipped down her stairs carrying a stack of towels, and who couldn't bear the thought of tending to guests on crutches, and luckily, thanks to only suffering a mild sprain, wouldn't have to.

His father had packed up most of his office, and Jason

had little to bring in. The wall of pictures and cards had been removed, each item carefully stacked in a box. It would take some time for Jason to rebuild a collection like that, and maybe it wouldn't happen, but it was a goal, and he'd never been shy about trying to walk in his father's footsteps. Melanie was out front in the lobby. It was her day off from the shop, even though she had an appointment after lunch with a new client who needed a dress made by August. She'd provided some preliminary ideas and Melanie had spent most of last night sketching away, and Jason had spent much of that time watching her do what she loved best.

He hung his framed diplomas on the hooks where his father's had been, and stood back to take in the space. The tree branches from the big elm filled most of the view, but if he looked down to the yard he could see the big sign welcoming patients to the Sawyer Family Clinic. It never had to come down now.

He set his laptop on the desk, deciding to transfer the files another day, or have Shelby do it, as he knew she guarded those carefully, along with the lollipops and the fish tank and all the other traditions that made this office more than just a place to work.

He dropped into the leather swivel chair and adjusted it to his height. Though his father would never admit it, Jason was a full two inches taller than him now, but even still, it felt like he was always looking up to him.

The drawers had been cleared out with the exception of patient records, which were locked. Jason opened the top drawer of the desk to be sure his father had left a spare set of keys, and frowned when he saw a picture frame resting in its center.

He pulled it out, smiling as his father's face came into view. He was young, about Jason's age, leaner in build, his head still covered with hair. He was standing in front of the clinic, next to the big welcome sign out of front, his arm around a pretty blonde woman who wore a shirtdress and pearls.

It was the day he had opened the clinic, Jason realized. The day he had described. Their future was bright.

It still was.

Jason propped the photo on his desk under the window, beside his laptop, where he could always see it, and then he stood and walked into the lobby.

"I was just feeding the fish," Melanie said, but her eyes were round with guilt and there was a lollipop in her hand, one that was half-eaten.

"Come on," Jason said, taking her by the hand and leading her outside.

"Where are we going?" she asked, but followed him down the steps to the grass, stopping beside the big sign as he did.

"We're marking the occasion," he said, pulling her in tight as he held up his cell phone, hoping he was holding it at the right angle.

"To the clinic staying open?" she asked, grinning up at him.

He smiled down at her and then looked back up at the screen in his hand. "To that. And to so much more."

USA TODAY bestselling author Olivia Miles writes heartwarming women's fiction with a romantic twist. She lives just outside Chicago with her husband, young daughter, and two ridiculously pampered pups. *Still the One* is her twentieth novel.

Visit Olivia's website at www.OliviaMilesBooks.com to learn more.

49472428R00139

Made in the USA
Lexington, KY
22 August 2019